"You were pregnant when I left," Hudson stated.

"Only about a month. I didn't know. I wasn't going to beg you to stay with me because I was pregnant. I was just being the selfish, privileged girl you said I was."

"And all the years since... I can't... It doesn't matter right now. We have to find her."

"I know. And I didn't intend to tell you until afterward, so you wouldn't be distracted...but with your friends looking into things...I didn't want you to hear it from them."

"I know why you made the choices you did back then. But all these years... How long have you known I was back?"

"Six months. When Hope got so bothered that she didn't have family, I thought about telling her about you. But I couldn't take the chance that you'd walk away from her..."

"You took her to see your parents instead."

"They're my family."

"And they really don't know I'm her father?"

"No one does."

They shared a daughter. But in giving him that news, Amanda had severed the bond they'd shared.

"I can't forgive you for this."

"I know."

Dear Reader,

Welcome to Sierra's Web! If this is your first time with this firm of experts, I hope you fall in love. If you're back for more, I'm so, so glad you wanted to spend more time with me here.

I'm a strong believer in one's ability to learn and to grow to effect change in our lives, and in part, that's this story. The characters are fictional, the events are fictional and yet the real story, to me, is very true. It's a second chance story. Love found two people when they didn't know what they needed to know. They didn't know what they didn't know. They thought they knew. And they made choices that tore them apart.

Love has a way, though. It finds us when we least expect it, in ways we least suspect. Question is, will we know what we need to know, will we have learned, can we be willing to understand and give someone another chance with our deepest selves? Will we have the courage to accept love's gifts?

And can a man find his abducted daughter in time to meet her?

Sierra's Web: a nationally renowned firm of experts; friends since college; solving crimes, puzzles and family dilemmas, too. Sierra's Web: a brand-new TTQ series with more chapters of the series coming in 2022.

Tara Taylor

TRACKING HIS SECRET CHILD

Tara Taylor Quinn

HARLEQUIN
ROMANTIC
SUSPENSE

HARLEQUIN®
ROMANTIC SUSPENSE™

Recycling programs
for this product may
not exist in your area.

ISBN-13: 978-1-335-73805-9

Tracking His Secret Child

Copyright © 2022 by TTQ Books LLC

For questions and comments about the quality of this book,
please contact us at CustomerService@Harlequin.com.

Harlequin Enterprises ULC
22 Adelaide St. West, 41st Floor
Toronto, Ontario M5H 4E3, Canada
www.Harlequin.com

Printed in U.S.A.

A *USA TODAY* bestselling author of one hundred novels in twenty languages, **Tara Taylor Quinn** has sold more than seven million copies. Known for her intense emotional fiction, Ms. Quinn's novels have received critical acclaim in the UK and most recently from Harvard. She is a recipient of the Readers' Choice Award and has appeared often on local and national TV, including *CBS Sunday Morning*.

For TTQ offers, news and contests, visit www.tarataylorquinn.com!

Books by Tara Taylor Quinn

Harlequin Romantic Suspense

Sierra's Web

Tracking His Secret Child

The Coltons of Colorado

Colton Countdown

Where Secrets are Safe

Her Detective's Secret Intent
Shielded in the Shadows
Falling for His Suspect

The Coltons of Grave Gulch

Colton's Killer Pursuit

Visit the Author Profile page at Harlequin.com for more titles.

To Drake—the world is yours, little man, and your tribe will help you navigate it every step of the way. Mima loves you very much!

Chapter 1

Sitting in his luxury condominium overlooking Tempe Town Lake, Hudson Warner frowned, but didn't look away from the half circle of screens installed on his desk. He'd just found his way into the dark web, using his IT expertise to investigate the computer dating record of an unfaithful spouse, and intended to snag the screen shots he needed, close out and go take another shower, as if he could wash the images out of his mind.

Sierra's Web, the firm of experts he'd founded with six of his college friends, had clients all over the country and took all kinds of jobs, but there were some he didn't enjoy. The phone rang. His business cell. A number he didn't recognize, at a time he didn't want to talk.

He let the call continue to voice mail and then, guilt kicking in, pressed to listen to the message. Just in case.

Urgent calls were common in the Sierra's Web world.

The message wasn't business and was one he'd never expected to receive.

"Hudson, oh, God, is that you? Please let it be you. I'm so sorry to bother you, and here I am needing you to do something for me, but, oh, God, Hudson, please call me." The voice was female. Clearly panicked. And maybe even containing tears.

It wasn't identified. And a new message beeped.

He pressed to listen.

"Hudson, I'm sorry. This is Amanda. Amanda Smith. Please…please, just call."

The hand holding his phone dropped to his desk. Hudson stared at it.

She'd rattled off a number. He could get it just as easily from his call log. Hit Call straight from there without even dialing.

Did he really want to do that? The door to that volatile period of his life had been closed a long time.

Opening long-shut doors usually didn't bring forth sunshine. Quite the opposite. And while he spent his life walking into other people's darkness in an attempt to help them rediscover their light, he wasn't up for delving into his own deep holes.

Hudson, please.

She'd never begged. Even when her selfishness had forced him to walk out on her, she hadn't begged him not to go.

She'd wished him well, as he recalled.

Of course, those fourteen-year-old memories were sketchy from lack of use. He accessed them rarely. And only when some reminder sprang up before he could block it.

Please, please…

What the hell.

She never begged.

And he'd worked hard to get her out of his system, lest they both be destroyed. No, maybe just to save himself.

What. The. Hell.

They'd been eighteen, he reaching that milestone six months before her. He'd been handed a miracle in the form of a full scholarship to an elite university he'd applied to with no hope at all. He'd taken the only chance he was going to get to make something great of his life.

Coming from foster care and then a children's home, he hadn't had much at his back. Or on his back, either, other than some hand-me-down clothes. And now, look at him—someone who people called when they desperately needed help.

Please let it be you.

There'd been no mistaking the desperation in her voice.

At home, pacing her spacious, sun-infused kitchen, Amanda didn't know what to do. Where to go. The police had told her stay put.

She couldn't just sit there. And hope.

Hope…oh, God, Hope…

Where was her baby girl? What was happening to her? Blocking the vision that immediately sprang to mind—her beautiful thirteen-year-old in tears, or worse—she shook her head. Paced faster. Harder.

Just in the kitchen. The rest of the house…she couldn't handle it yet…

Oh, God…

The phone she clutched tightly in one hand vibrated a second before it rang, and she immediately pulled it up. *Hope?*

The number didn't belong to her daughter.

But the voice on the other end was still welcome.

"Hudson?" He'd called. He'd really called? Tears sprang to her eyes again. He'd called. Feeling like she'd just had her first ray of hope since the school had phoned an hour before, she said, "Hudson?" a bit shakily, and then sniffed.

"Yeah. What's going on?" His voice held urgency. And she started to cry harder. And forced herself to stop. Hope needed her.

Needed him. Though neither of them knew about the other.

A deep, dark secret that was going to be exposed because she'd called him. And she couldn't worry about that. He could hate her. Hope could, too.

As long as Hope was safe.

"My thirteen-year-old daughter, Hope—she's missing, Hudson…" Breaking off as a sob bubbled up, she forced herself to take a small breath. To calm herself. "She didn't show up in her second-period class and hasn't been seen or heard from since…" Going on two hours now.

Fear washed over her. Weakening her. The world felt surreal.

An awful she'd never imagined…

"Have you called the police?" His voice…it was deeper. More mature. And still swept through her, leaving warmth in its wake. Thawing her chilled blood.

Like the first time they'd met. She'd been Hope's age. The police had just come and carted her wealthy, respected parents off to jail. And she'd been taken to a children's home to spend the night. To stay until other arrangements were made for her. Four years later, she'd still been there.

A person no one wanted to touch because she still associated with her imprisoned parents.

"Yes, there's a team of detectives. They're doing all they can," she said, shaking her head again as she paced around the table. And then stood at the bay window looking out over the colorful vegetation in her perfectly landscaped backyard. And on to the pool. Hope loved the water, and Amanda remembered watching her long blond hair floating behind her as she swam.

"They've...they said they have to get into her computer. They're going to put their techie on it, but I..." She couldn't go back now. She'd called him. "I've looked you up, Hud, and I know what you do, and that you're local, and please, will you come? Go over her computer? If there's something..." God, no "...hidden there, I know you'll find it the fastest. They say the first twenty-four hours are the most critical."

Silence fell on the line, and she held her breath. He'd come. He had to come.

Opening her mouth to tell him why he would come, she didn't get a word out before he said, "I'm on my way."

"My address?"

"I've got it," he told her, repeating it for her. "I just looked you up. You're in real estate..."

A broker. With a team of licensed professionals who

worked for her. And awards on her walls. None of which mattered at all anymore. She gave him the gate code to get into her community.

"The police think she ran away," she said, running a hand through her own long blond hair in a pathetic attempt to ease the ache in her head. One that had already spread through the rest of her body. Turning from the brightness at the window, she faced the double built-in ovens she'd been so proud to own. "But I know she didn't," she said, hearing a door shut through the line, and then a car door slam. In another few seconds his car's audio system had picked up the call.

"You're about forty minutes from here," she told him.

"I'm not at the office. I'm coming from home. I'm in Tempe. I'll be there in twenty."

He paused. "Is her father there with you?" His question shot bullets through her.

"No. I'm a single parent," she said when she could, swallowing the lump in her throat.

"Any chance she's just playing hooky?" he asked. She wished she could hold on to that hope, but knew better.

"Hope's a good kid, Hudson." She wanted him to know that. "We're…close. She tells me everything, even if she thinks it's going to make me mad. No way she'd just act out like this. She's…not selfish like I was. She'd be aware about making everyone worry."

Because Amanda had raised her to be aware. No way she'd let Hope grow up as self-centered as her parents had raised her.

"I'm scared, Hudson. I…took her to meet my parents

not long ago. I'm scared to death that this has something to do with them."

He'd get it. Completely. He'd lived through those
awful first months in the children's home with her.
Shielding her from the news, from kids at her new
school…and explaining to her the mass of white-collar
crimes her parents had knowingly committed, robbing
hundreds of people out of their life savings.

People who'd thrown their hate and anger at her more
than once.

"That's why I need you on her computer," she told
him. "If they've got her doing something for them,
you'll be able to follow innocuous-seeming trails. Multiple encryptions. Figure it all out. You'll notice if anything that might look like an adolescent site to most is
really a cover for something else…"

She'd read multiple articles about Sierra's Web. He
and his firm of experts from all different fields had
made national news more than once, too. His reputation and honors had grown far larger than hers had.

And what if Hope had gone looking for the father
she'd never met?

Choices Amanda had made at eighteen, after Hudson had walked out on her, piled up, until she started to
sink beneath their weight. She'd done what she thought
best—not just for herself. For the first time ever, she'd
consciously, knowingly, put someone else first.

And she'd robbed her daughter of half her legacy,
too. She hadn't realized how much Hope would need to
know where she came from…how much not knowing
had bothered her daughter, at least not until the discus-
sion they'd had six months before.

Which was why Amanda had finally told her the truth about her parents—Hope's grandparents. And then, at her insistence, taken her to see them, each in their own sections, on visiting day. Once a month for the past five months.

Hudson's voice broke into her thoughts. "Let me get off and call the police. I'll offer to help with the investigation," he continued, as though thinking aloud. Something she remembered from the past. Him saying his thoughts out loud. "Normally they call us in, but I'll see what I can do. You got a name of the detectives on the case?"

Jeanine Crosby and Steven Wedbush. She gave him their numbers. Hardly able to stand. Weak with relief. *And fear.*

"Thank you," she told him. But he'd already hung up. All business.

And she was fine with that.

Falling down to a chair at the table, she buried her head in her arms and let herself cry. To get it out. Because once Hudson arrived, there'd be no time for her at all. He was going to search, and she was going to be right there, thinking clearly, giving him every piece of information she had, helping him figure out passwords or anything else he might need to know.

She'd show him her bank accounts, and Hope's, so he could see that she wasn't anything like her parents.

She'd show him pictures, health records. Anything. Everything.

Sitting up, she started to think rationally. Grabbing the magnetic notepad off the refrigerator, she began making a list of anything that Hudson, or the police, might need to know to find Hope.

She'd already given the detectives a list of her daughter's friends, teammates and activities, and the church they attended.

But there was more.

There'd been that boy who'd asked her to the winter dance.

And the time she'd gone to an inline skate park with a group of friends.

Things came rushing back, and she took them all down as fast as she could. Hope was out there...most likely in danger...and she needed Amanda to be strong.

To be there for her.

She needed Hudson, too. And he was coming.

Hope would be overjoyed to know that. Amanda tried to picture Hope's expression when Amanda told her who he was.

And couldn't yet.

It was enough that he was coming.

He was going to help her find Hope, just because she'd asked.

She knew that she wasn't going to escape the inevitable, though. She'd broken too many years of silence, and there would be no going back.

Whether he found out immediately or not. Whether he found Hope or not.

And whether he hated her or not.

She was going to have to introduce him to the daughter he didn't know he had.

Chapter 2

Amanda's daughter was thirteen. His ex-girlfriend hadn't mourned him long. She'd gotten pregnant within a year of his leaving.

But apparently that guy hadn't stuck around, either.

At eighteen, Hudson knew he had been her first lover. And he'd felt…trapped.

Not by her. Or her love. But by the life he'd pictured, settling down, marrying, as a high school graduate with only himself to rely on for any success he might find. No way Amanda, who, while sensitive and big hearted, had only thought of life in terms of how it affected her, would have had the emotional strength, ability, or maybe willingness, to help him with his own goals.

She'd relied on him to be her strength.

But hadn't given him the same privilege.

Maybe, if he'd been independently wealthy, had familial support, or she had, he'd have stuck around…

Based on case history with him and women, probably not.

And none of that mattered a whit. Just chatter taking up brain space until he could get his hands on the child's computer. He itched to do so, had already spoken with the police in Chandler—the valley city in which Amanda lived—and received an acceptance of his offer to work with them pro bono. His reputation preceded him in terms of having access to a potential crime scene—the computer. And he wasn't going to lose time dealing with the necessary funding appropriation bids, approvals and paperwork required for a paying gig.

He wasn't going to waste time in a backwash of emotion, either, he told himself as he pulled into the wide drive leading up to Amanda's garage door and saw her come out the front door at the same time. She'd obviously been watching for him.

He recognized her immediately. Her body had matured, her curves more noticeable, but those high cheekbones framed by layers of soft blond hair—she was still wearing it long and straight, tucked behind her ears. And the blue eyes, as she drew closer…they hadn't changed at all.

Their mixture of beauty, mystery and neediness drew him just as they had at fourteen. He'd seen her sitting in a chair in the house mother's office her first night at the home, and that gaze had implored him to get her out of the hell she'd fallen into.

He hadn't known the details at the time, but he'd

learned them pretty quickly. And had appointed himself the girl's savior. Having been in foster homes, and then the children's home, since he was five, he knew the lay of the land. Could tutor her in the dos and don'ts of life with only yourself to rely on.

The obviously expensive black pants and matching jacket she was wearing reminded him of the fancy clothes she'd come in with way back when. The ones she'd cried over when she'd grown out of them and had to accept the secondhand garments they got to choose out of the regular donations. Luckily for her, sometimes the hand-me-downs had had designer labels.

She reached out toward him as she approached. Thinking she might be about to hug him, he reached out a hand, which she took with both of hers. Looked up into his eyes. And started to tear up.

As though none of those years had passed. She'd always shared all of her emotions with him.

"Hud…I can't thank you enough for coming…" she was saying, and all he wanted to do was get to the computer. To find the kid. And…

Just find the kid.

He almost told her she looked good. Which, overall, she did. Great, in fact. But not something you told a panic-stricken woman. Not something he should even be noticing.

"It's just so good to see you," she said, holding on to his hand, giving it a squeeze and then letting go.

"It's good to see you, too." Surprising how much he meant those words.

And all the more reason to get to the computer, bring her daughter back to her and get the hell out of there.

* * *

So ungodly strange to be walking Hudson Warner into Hope's room. He'd been there in her mind many times in the two years since she and their daughter had moved in there. But fantasy and reality weren't ever supposed to meet.

And her child wasn't ever supposed to go missing.

As soon as he entered the room, he made a bee-line for the desktop computer on Hope's student desk. Didn't even seem to glance at the rest of the room. He had the machine on and booting up before she'd caught her breath. She told him the password. Stood there, as though her presence was somehow necessary. Fighting a new spate of tears as he lowered his five-foot-eleven frame into Hope's chair.

His dark hair was just as thick, but not as unruly. Cut just above the collar, his trim looked like the rest of him, expensive. Casually expensive. His dark dress pants could have entered any boardroom. Not so much the gray, slightly wrinkled, untucked button-down shirt.

"You know her social media passwords?" He'd turned in the chair and her gaze locked on his. The deep brown of his eyes…they'd been making promises since the first time she'd seen him. Promising to be there for her. Or, at least, promising that everything was going to be okay.

And, she supposed, up until that morning, it had been. She'd made it through her years at the home, made it through his desertion, through single parenthood, college, real estate testing. She'd made it. And everything had been just fine.

"Magnet8," she said. And then added, "Magnet was

a rescue toy poodle we got when she was four. We lost her a couple of years ago."

"Eight is for how many years you had her?" A lucky guess, but…

"No, it's her favorite number." Something a parent would know.

He'd called up the first website. With fingers clicking and screens flashing so quickly in front of him that she couldn't even make out what it all was, she figured he probably wasn't listening, anyway.

Conflicted, she hovered, looking around the room. Perching on the edge of the bed for a bit. She should call someone to come sit with her. After all, she had friends who would rush right over. They would be calling as soon as they heard that Hope was gone.

If they heard. There was still hope she'd come walking in the door—which was the reason the police wanted Amanda to stay put. So she'd be there at home if Hope showed up. There was also a chance her daughter would end up back at school before the day was out, to catch the bus home. Detective Crosby had given her several scenarios to think about.

Mostly so she didn't go straight to worst-case scenario, she was sure. Right to the parent's worst nightmare: a young girl, being abducted. *No.* She had to stop. Had to have hope. For Hope.

Hope for Hope. From the moment she found out she was having a girl, that had been her motto.

The computer screen was lines of letters and numbers. Hudson scrolled, clicked, opened new windows, scrolled and clicked some more.

He acted like she wasn't there, but she stayed. In case

he had another question. After five minutes of listening to clicking and silence, she retrieved the list she'd made while waiting for him. Laid it on the desk, but didn't interrupt.

He glanced at it, and then back at the screen.

It didn't seem as though he'd found anything yet, but just like with a doctor's exam, you had to just endure and wait until the examiner was done and ready to give you the rundown. The final verdict. Even if it meant more tests.

Her gaze fell on a picture of her and Hope at Disneyland, taken the previous year. They were both wearing Mickey Mouse ears and laughing. The trip had been at Hope's request and had been inarguably the most carefree, enjoyable time of Amanda's life.

The pang of guilt that hit her as she looked at those smiling faces was new. And couldn't be denied. Hudson hadn't had a chance to build a single memory with his daughter. He'd deserted Amanda. Made it clear that he wanted a clean break—said it was for the best, for both of them. He'd had his reasons.

Some good.

It wasn't until two months later that she'd known she was pregnant.

She remembered some of his last words to her. The ones that had rung the loudest and hung around the longest were that while he'd slept with her, he'd never promised her a future. But that hadn't been the worst of it. He'd said that she needed to learn to take care of herself, rather than always expecting someone else to take care of her.

The words had stung so bad, she could feel their bite still.

He'd told her that before she could expect someone to be in a relationship with her, she needed to learn how to give as well as take.

In some ways those words had hurt far worse than anything her parents' actions had inflicted on her. Partially because he'd been the one saying them. But also because their truth had been clear.

The pain those words had left behind still lingered within her. Had been driving her since he'd walked away to catch the one-way flight out of Phoenix that his fancy Arkansas school had paid for.

And it was that pain that was going to drive her to tell him the truth about Hope's parentage now that he was back in their lives. Her reasons for keeping Hope to herself back then had been very clear at the time. And were no longer valid.

Another guilt ate at her as she stared at that picture of what had seemed like a perfect time. A perfect memory. For six months, Hope had been struggling with a need to know where she came from. So Amanda had taken her daughter to meet her imprisoned grandparents when her own father had been just across town.

And yet, looking at Hudson as he bent with such single focus over the computer screen, without glancing around at all to learn anything about the child for whom he looked, she'd had good reason not to tell Hope about Hudson.

If the man had rejected her…wanted nothing to do with her…if he'd walked away…

Amanda knew how deeply that pain cut. She wasn't going to let the man inflict it upon her daughter.

So she'd tell him before she told Hope. Pray to God she got a chance to tell Hope.

Yes. Praying for Hope. That had to be her sole focus. No reason to tell Hudson yet that he had a personal connection to the case. His daughter needed his full focus on finding her first.

"Does she have a cell phone?" He was still clicking, scrolling.

Amanda stood. Walked forward. "Yes. But she doesn't have it with her. She's not allowed to take it to school. Detective Crosby has it."

Without turning, he pulled a cell phone out of his shirt pocket, dialed, and within a minute had received an affirmative on a request for the cell phone. An officer was bringing it over.

"She has other social media accounts?" he asked.

"Yes." He opened a well-known website, typed in the same password she'd given him for the first account without asking for it, and got right in. "I've noticed she uses the same password everywhere I've looked," he said. "That's not good. She needs to change them up."

And Amanda would be quite happy to see that she did so. If she got her back. They had to get her back first!

Tears sprang to her eyes again. She didn't blame Hudson. He was doing his job. And she wanted him as focused as he was.

She just couldn't believe…

She'd recognize a screen, and then there'd be a bit of typing, and more lines of code would appear. Pages of them. Hudson would highlight some, right-click, then move on. He switched from screen to screen so rapidly sometimes she couldn't keep track of them.

And kept thinking of Hope out in the real world, not there in her room, safe, where she belonged. Like she hadn't wanted to leave the kitchen earlier, she couldn't make herself get up and leave the room. Her whole heart was represented there. Hudson, the boy who'd grown into a man by her side and kept her whole and alive through what she'd thought would be the worst tragedy of her life. And Hope, who'd given her hope, and purpose outside herself, from the second she knew of her conception. Hope, who'd been patient while Amanda grew into a woman worthy of having her.

But had she been worthy? She hadn't been able to keep her safe…

She jumped when her phone rang, and her heart started to pound. Grabbing the cell out of her jacket pocket, she answered immediately.

Listened. Nodded.

Wiped at the tears that just wouldn't stop coming that morning.

She heard Detective Crosby's words, but couldn't think. Couldn't process. "Are you sure?" she heard herself ask.

The rest of the phone call was a blur. Platitudes, empty promises, an assurance that everyone was doing all they could, an admonishment to stay strong and a vow from the detective to stay in touch.

"What is it?"

Hudson's voice pulled her back into the now. Into being present. Pulled her out of the void she'd slipped into through her helplessness.

How did one stay strong when all one could do was sit and do nothing? Strength required action…

"Amanda?" She glanced up at the no-nonsense tone. Met that brown gaze. And just as she had all those years before when she'd first met that gaze, she held on.

"They have her on tape leaving school," she said. "It was between first and second period. She slipped out a side door and simply walked out of view." She couldn't believe it. Hope had left of her own free will?

"They know the direction she took, but she's got a three-hour head start…"

Police were canvassing the area, but Amanda had heard the doubt in Jeanine Crosby's tone to her. If Hope had run away, they'd still look for her, but not with the urgency they were currently using. Not with the same manpower.

And wherever she'd gone, Hope needed them. Amanda knew that her daughter would not have just run away. She knew it. But if no one else believed her, how long would they keep looking?

"Even if there was a boy, which I seriously doubt based on some of our recent conversations, she'd come to me first. At least give me a chance to hear her out, no matter who he was. She isn't afraid of me, Hud. Because I'm always fair with her. She trusts me to give her her way anytime I can, and on the other side of it, she trusts me to keep her safe. When I say no, she sometimes asks why, but she doesn't argue. Or go behind my back. The one time when she did go behind my back— to sneak a chocolate bunny out of the refrigerator after I'd told her she'd had enough—she came to me while the chocolate was still goo in her mouth.

"I told her then that as long as she came to me, we'd make whatever trouble she'd gotten into right. That I'd always listen to understand and would always be fair. She's reminded me of that a few times when we've clashed and she's determined to do something against my better judgment. She's a rare individual…an old soul in a young body…" As she talked, it occurred to her that she was babbling a bit—and also doing what she'd said she was going to do. She was introducing Hudson Warner to his daughter.

She just hoped to God that he'd get to meet Hope in person.

And that when he found out who she was, he'd want her.

Chapter 3

Hudson knew within minutes that Hope was more than just a young teen doing homework and going to school. While her overall computer password was used multiple times—a definite security no-no—the girl had curious encryptions set up and seemingly no need for them. At the very least, she was a smart kid, a computer-savvy one.

While the discovery might have amused him at another time, the encryptions, sometimes two and three deep, were frustrating the hell out of him, slowing him down, as he attempted to get a sense of everything on her hard drive as quickly as possible. At first, he'd thought himself onto something big, but he'd fight his way through the somewhat simple encryptions and they'd lead nowhere of any import.

She was experimenting. Learning. Solving puzzles. He could see the evolution.

And a peek at the personality behind it—something he was purposely avoiding. As he always did. He couldn't let the human factor sway his perspective. He was like a scientist who needed an unbiased examination of data to see where it led. If he went in with preconceived notions, looking for something in particular, he could miss something vital and not even know it.

After he had his first look, he'd start asking more questions, try to get into the head of the content creator. You could get *more* personally involved, but you couldn't get less. Once the information was in his brain, his first impression would be tainted.

And…in this particular case…with Amanda's child… he had to take extra precautions where bias was concerned. His curiosity about the child she'd raised, apparently alone.

"Has she ever had contact with her father?" he asked. Hope wouldn't be the first child to find a birth parent behind another parent's back.

"No. She doesn't know who he is. And since he's not named on her birth certificate, she'd have no way of finding out."

A one-night stand, then?

Or someone else who found himself incapable of constantly tending to her neediness? While she'd clearly made a good life for herself, even just based on the job she held and neighborhood she lived in, she'd had a lot of years between the birth and the child's disappearance in which to grow up.

Definitely not information pertaining to his current

job scope. Now that he knew there were no paternal names for which to be watching...

Letters flashed by. He backed up. Looked at them again. He'd been scrolling through coding, but recognized a name in a text code.

George Smythe.

Hope had not only searched her grandfather's name—understandable, seeing that Amanda had just recently taken her to meet the man. Hope had searched what she could about his case. But she'd delved deeper. Searched the man's associates, too.

The deeper he went into her search results, the more he found. Random things.

Including financial institutions accessed during a certain time sequence. Interesting—especially for a teenager.

Those dated back four months. But there could be more. He had months' worth of information to get through.

Turning around, facing the room, he saw Amanda sitting on the side of her daughter's double bed, the frilly spread perfectly fitting his memory of Amanda.

"How long ago exactly did you first take your daughter to meet your father?" he asked. She'd said recently. Had had some concerns. Did she know more than she was telling him?

Needing him, not the police, to find out what was on that computer so she could do damage control?

If she was using him in some nefarious scheme...

"Five months."

The beginning of Hope's unusual computer activity dated back the same amount of time.

His heart sank.

* * *

Things were getting sticky already. She had to tell him everything. Most particularly the fact that his daughter knew nothing about him. Because no one did. Amanda had never told anyone. Period.

I can't. Not without telling him first.

And being a girl who'd just left a children's home—albeit a wonderful, privately run one that ran a huge thrift store to help self-support, and to give teenage residents a chance to earn—to start a new job as a receptionist at a veterinary clinic, whose parents were in prison, and who was a virtual pariah to anyone in her past life, keeping secrets had been astonishingly simple. There'd been no one in her life who'd been curious enough to press her into spilling her truths.

Even her doctor had been new to her. The home's pediatrician services were no longer available to her and not appropriate, either. A simple *the father is no longer in my life* had been enough to keep anyone from asking more.

Horribly sad, how easy it had been. And a blessing, too.

But for the moment, she had to tell him what she knew about her parents. From the moment she'd heard Hope was missing, she'd had a sick feeling in her gut that it had to do with her mom and dad somehow.

She never should have told her about them. Or taken her to meet them...

"Hope was struggling." She started in slowly, trying to pick and choose what to say immediately, and what to save to discuss when time wasn't so much of the essence. "It's always just been the two of us, and after having a family history lesson at school, a look at the diversity of class backgrounds, she was consumed with her lack of belonging, her lack of familial support beyond just me. Up until that point I hadn't told her about her grandparents. She knew that I grew up in a children's home. And that I've been on my own since I was eighteen. Up until six months ago, that had been enough. She used to say she liked our family. The way we were always together. And the fact that she got me all to herself.

"My folks were from Scottsdale, not Chandler, and Smith is such a common name…"

"And they spelled it Smythe." He gave it the long *I* pronunciation that she'd dropped, at the suggestion of social workers, before she'd started public school.

"I never should have told her about them," she said now. "She obsessed over them. I'd told her about the parents I'd known and loved, and then explained that they'd made some bad business decisions, trying to spare her, but she kept asking questions. I know she looked them up on the internet. She told me after she'd done so, and we had frank conversations then. About them. About my transition from the life I'd known to the one she'd heard about. She seemed to calm down then, and I thought we were through with it until she suddenly wanted to meet them."

"I'm assuming they're being housed here in the valley?"

She nodded. "Just like it was in the past, part of their plea agreement was that they could be kept in the same city, and close to me." He'd known Amanda had consistently gone to see them when she'd been a teenager.

Had seemed to be waiting each time she'd come back

and had silently sat beside her while she'd sobbed every time, too.

"Did they know about her?"

"Of course. I saw them every month. I couldn't very well hide an advanced pregnancy from them." When she'd been younger, she hadn't had a lot of choice about the visitations. As an adult, she'd come to terms with the fact that while she didn't condone what they'd done, and would vote to keep them incarcerated because of it, she loved them for the parents they'd been to her. For the good parts of them. "But I'd never taken her to see them. I went when she was at the babysitter's, and later, school."

Her mom had cried the whole of Hope's first visit. Even her father had been teary-eyed. Neither of them had tried to explain their behavior to their granddaughter. They'd spent the entire hour asking Hope about herself. And telling her how happy they were to have finally met her. And they let her know that they'd been loving her her entire life, recounting different things Amanda had told them. Referencing pictures of her that Amanda had brought over the years.

Being a child of convicts wasn't an easy thing. Being their granddaughter had to be equally tough. Maybe even more so because it left her with very little sense of solid family support.

"I never felt good about taking her to see them," she said. "I should have waited until she was eighteen…"

But life was about tough calls. She'd been afraid someone from her past could appear out of nowhere. Afraid, as Hope grew older, that she'd see Amanda's silences as lies…

Just as she was going to see the lie about her father.

Most particularly if she got to meet him and saw what Amanda had deprived her of all those years...

Sitting there with him, she hated herself a bit for that, and wouldn't blame Hope for hating her, too. But after Hudson had walked out on her...he hadn't seemed real.

She'd been alone. A mess. Needing to prove to herself that she could fix the things he'd said about her. That she could love unselfishly. Make something of herself without someone else taking care of her. She'd had other fears, too...

None of which mattered at the moment.

Hudson had turned back to the computer and was typing. She thought back over their conversation. "Why did you ask the exact timing of Hope's visit with my father?" If she wasn't in shock and consumed by fear, she'd have caught on to that right away.

"I saw some things on her search engine. You've now explained them."

Good, then. She was helping. Doing something.

She had to do something. She was no longer the person who sat around waiting for others to do for her. Hadn't been that woman for a long, long time.

Standing, she opened the door to her daughter's closet. Intending to occupy herself somehow. Straightening things on hangers if nothing else. She needed to touch Hope's things. To be busy with them. To have them ready for her to come back.

And to stay close in case Hudson had any more questions.

She had her cell phone with her. If there was going to be a ransom call, she'd get it wherever she was.

But while she was comfortable, she definitely wasn't in the upper-class financial bracket. Wasn't successful enough to warrant a ransom due to the kidnapping of a thirteen-year-old girl.

Which left taking her for another reason…

A sob rose within her, and she forced herself to take the next article of clothing on the rack, a sweater, and reposition it so it hung evenly. Hope was good about hanging up her things. She just tended to be more in a hurry to get the job done than to do it well.

Not a general rule for her, though. Mostly Hope gave her best to everything she did. She truly was a great kid.

"Amanda…"

Turning, another sweater in hand, she saw Hudson's frown as he glanced her way and then back at the computer. "Yeah?"

"I've followed an encrypted trail here to what looks like a series of numbers that could be from a foreign bank account. I recognize the routing number, but it's jumbled in the middle of a long numerical series that otherwise makes no sense to me. Do you recognize any of this?"

Shaking, she moved closer to him. Looked at the line he'd highlighted and panicked when none of it looked the least bit familiar to her. Only the warmth emanating from his skin kept her somewhat able to focus and allow rational thought.

"Why would she have that?" she asked, trying to understand something that was so far out of the realm of possibility that it didn't seem real.

His only answer was a half shake of the head as he

typed, brought up a couple more screens in quick succession and typed some more.

"No account number apparent yet," he announced a short time later as he picked up his phone and then spoke to Detective Crosby. Amanda knew because he'd called the detective by name. He appeared to answer some questions after his initial disclosure, based on the one- and two-word responses she heard. Then said he'd keep looking and be in touch.

Putting his phone down, he continued to work at the computer, moving quickly through screens, as he said, "They're following up on your concern regarding your parents."

She nodded. She felt avenged. And yet…more scared than ever. It had been nearly two decades since her parents had swindled so many people out of more money than she could really comprehend. She'd suspected they could be behind the kidnapping…but only because she'd been so hurt by them when she'd been Hope's age, not because she'd really thought they still had some ties that could hurt them. Not nearly so much time later.

"Crosby went through the old case files this morning," Hudson said, turning in his seat to face her as the computer screen showed a continuous circle going round and round. With the half-hung sweater still in hand, she sank down to Hope's bed. She was not going to fall apart.

This wasn't about her. It was about helping Hope.

"Apparently there was a fairly substantial amount of money that was never accounted for," he told her. "Your parents' ties to it weren't irrefutable, and they claimed they had no knowledge of it. Since they were, as part of their plea agreement, turning over everything they had to the government, including some dealings of which the prosecutors had been otherwise unaware, there was no cause to doubt their assertions."

She could feel the blood leaving her face. "There's still money out there? And you think Hope has something to do with it?"

His gaze didn't leave hers.

And she knew.

"You think someone's using her to access it."

He didn't confirm her conclusion. But he didn't deny it, either. He did, however, look her straight in the eye as he asked, "Do you know anything about it?"

"No!" She couldn't believe he was asking. Until she suddenly saw what he did. A woman from his past calling him out of the blue. Fearing that her daughter's disappearance had to do with an old crime for which her parents were serving life in prison. The fact that she'd been visiting them every month since their incarcerations. And had just taken her daughter to meet them.

And the detective…she'd have to be looking at Amanda, too.

Horror spread through her in waves of chills and heat. Making her nauseous. She didn't look away from him, though. She couldn't.

Hudson was a rock upon which she stood in the midst of turbulent waters.

"I swear to God, Hudson, I knew nothing about this. Do you honestly think I'd have taken my daughter to see them if I'd known? If I'd thought there was anything from the past that would come back to haunt her? It's been so many years. I thought it was safe!"

It hadn't been safe. Her daughter was missing.

And now Amanda herself was a suspect?

She'd thought she'd learned how to take care of herself.

And others. Leading a team of professionals who learned from her how to treat clients fairly in the business world. And who, with the aid of her adamant ethical practices, gained leverage and financial success through her.

She'd been standing on her own, solving her own problems, providing a good life for herself and her daughter for more than fourteen years, if you counted the nine months of pregnancy.

She'd been so certain she'd succeeded in life.

And there she was, with her daughter in imminent danger, sitting with a sweater on her lap, helpless and needy once again.

Chapter 4

Hudson believed her. For all her possible shortcomings, Amanda had never lied to him. Maybe because of what her parents had done, or maybe because they'd managed to not pass on their own greed to their child, Amanda Smythe had always been black-and-white when it came to following the rules.

That had been part of the reason they'd waited until her eighteenth birthday to have sex. A lot of kids their age who were dating had been sleeping with each other during their high school years, but not them. Amanda had been adamant about making them wait because rules at the home had said no sex while she was underage.

Of course, that had all been long ago.

He had no idea what kind of businesswoman she'd grown into.

And still, as he sat there, looking into those wide,

pure blue eyes, he believed her. And knew, too, that she was going to have a tougher time of convincing the detectives of her innocence. Unless he could find something on either her or Hope's computer that could exonerate her.

Something wasn't right. No way was it normal for a kid's computer to have foreign bank account routing numbers on it. If he was going to help either Amanda or her daughter, he had to figure out what was going on.

Their only lead at the moment was the possible bank account. But there could be more on Hope's computer. He had hours of work ahead of him.

And assuming their current theories were correct, then Hope's time could be more limited than other kidnapping-for-ransom victims. As soon as they had what they needed from her, her being alive was going to be nothing but a huge encumbrance. Other than the mysterious bank account, there was likely no money left to squeeze out.

"I need access to your computer, and I've got to see what else is here," he said, instilling calm into his tone. An assurance he didn't really feel. Falling into old habits with Amanda. Needing to wipe that lost and frightened look from her eyes. "And I need to follow what trail I can find regarding the routing number," he said. "Right now, it's all they've got to lead them to Hope."

Because far more important than foreign bank account and money concerns, far more important than what anyone thought Amanda did or didn't know about any of it, far more important than anything, was finding Hope.

He saw her nod. Noted the pallor of her skin. And turned his back.

He couldn't be her savior again.

But he was going to do everything in his power to help save her daughter.

Wrapping her mind around the idea that she was a possible suspect in her own daughter's disappearance distracted Amanda enough to calm her some. To keep her strong. She delivered her new laptop/tablet hybrid to Hudson immediately, lest he think she took time to erase anything from it, explaining that because her real estate job required her to be out with clients so much and her team needed her connected, the unit was the only device she used.

Detective Crosby called soon after that, letting her know that a forensic team was on their way to go through Hope's room. Feeling guilty for rearranging hangers, she went back to the kitchen, thought about a cup of tea. Called her top-producing agent to let her know that she wouldn't be in for the rest of the day. She didn't say why.

Hope's disappearance could make the news. She was praying for an Amber Alert. But at the moment, she couldn't bring herself to tell her friends or associates what was going on. She just couldn't wallow in their sympathy.

She had to deal with the situation, not expect others to coddle her through it.

What exactly did you do with yourself when you were handling something that provided no opportunity for action? Empty the dishwasher. It was her turn, after all. She fumbled with silverware, told herself to get a grip. She lifted a glass, caught it on the overhang, dropped it and felt a shattered shard hit her ankle.

Blinking back tears, she refused to stop. With the dishwasher door closed, she carefully picked up the big pieces and threw them away. Got her broom and dustpan out of the laundry room and swept up the rest. She reopened the dishwasher, lifted every item with deliberation and delivered them all to their proper places.

Like I hope my daughter will be delivered back to me.

Amanda jumped as the doorbell rang.

The forensic team. Her strength increased as she took the two-man team back to Hope's room. Things were happening. She was facilitating. She had to have purpose.

Seeing Hudson sitting at Hope's desk, both computer screens running side by side, helped. It even warmed some of the ice in her veins.

Phoenix and her surrounding sister valley cities were rarely cold. Temperatures that February Friday morning were up in the sixties. And still, she shivered as she left the room.

Hating that Hope's privacy was being violated, even while she welcomed anything that would help get her daughter safely home, she itched to get out *there*. To drive the streets looking for any sign of Hope.

The detectives had told her to stay home. But she wasn't a prisoner. Couldn't just sit there. If she left, though, would they think she was doing something nefarious? Part of a plan?

Male voices came from Hope's room. She couldn't

make out words, but she didn't think she heard Hudson. Nervous pains shot through her stomach.

They intensified almost to the point of crippling when a knock sounded on the front door. Practically tripping over her feet, Amanda hurried to answer it.

Hope? Please let it be Hope!

She barely found the wherewithal to look through the peephole first. And when she did, her burst of energy seeped out through her feet.

The detectives were back. Their expressions noncommittal, until she opened the door. Then they turned to a combination of serious and compassionate. Detective Jeanine Crosby stepped in first, her dark, shoulder-length hair softening her overall demeanor some. The rest of her, from the skinny black pants and pullover sweater to the black flats, gave an appearance of one who'd take on demons, and win without blinking.

Amanda wanted to be that strong. That capable. But she didn't ever see herself facing down bad guys without cringing.

Unless one of them had her daughter. Then she'd fight to the death without a second's thought.

"Can we have a seat?" Detective Wedbush, in brown dress pants, a shirt and tie, asked. The folded paper bag he had clasped under one arm made her uneasy.

To the point of feeling sick to her stomach.

She showed them to the family room sectional where she and Hope had stretched out—feet touching now and then on the ottoman—watching a family sitcom on television the night before. Now she was alone, perched on the edge of the short side of the couch.

Her hands clinging to each other, she eyed that brown

bag. And knew she didn't want the next minutes to happen. Grew more panicky because she couldn't stop them.

Please, God.

The sound of paper being moved filled her ears so loudly she couldn't hear anything else. "Does this belong to your daughter, Ms. Smith?" Wedbush asked. Just raw like that. No buildup.

She didn't want to look and couldn't help but stare at the tennis shoe in the man's gloved hand. Once her gaze landed there, she couldn't pull it away. Hope's pristine white tennis shoe with the pink *H* on the back heel. Half of the pair she'd monogrammed herself and only wore on the courts. To keep the bottoms clean so they didn't damage the surface of the court.

"They were tied to the strap of her book bag," she said. "She's been working with the high school tennis coach, hoping to make the girl's team as a freshman next year."

She was getting to the point that she gave Amanda a run for her money, and Amanda had trained with the best as a kid.

Her kid had only trained with her.

Amanda couldn't take her gaze off that shoe. Only one. She wanted to snatch it, hide it under her top, close to her heart where no one could see or touch it. Where it didn't symbolize anything but her daughter following in her footsteps and showing a natural aptitude for tennis.

But the shoe's missing counterpart was a problem. Where was it? The laces had been knotted together, knocking against the doorjamb as they'd gone out to the car to drive to school that morning.

"Amanda?"

Jeanine Crosby's voice came softly through a fog, gaining Amanda's attention. She looked at the detective before she could stop herself from letting go of the shoe. When she looked back, it was gone, hidden back in the bag. She watched Wedbush pull off the glove.

And was only then aware of the tears on her cheeks. "It's…hers," she reiterated. Told them about the book bag hitting the doorjamb that morning. And then, looking the female detective straight in the eye, asked, "Where did you find it?"

"The park on the other side of the wash behind the high school."

A park that, like many of the cultivated grassy areas in the desert valley, had been designed to be a runoff to keep water away from nearby buildings and neighborhoods during the monsoons. As a Realtor, Amanda knew that those washes were required by law. A developer had to plan for them, and provide them, to get a housing project approved.

She made herself breathe. Grabbed a tissue, tried to wipe her face and then clutched the wet, curled-up piece of softness in her palm. She said, "She's not allowed in that park. With the bus stop by the parking lot, it's become known as a place to get drugs."

She knew what the detectives were thinking. Amanda said it first. "Parents say that their kids wouldn't do drugs. Or join a gang. Or get into any other kind of trouble of which they're unaware, and I'm not saying Hope is perfect, but I know she wouldn't do drugs. Or simply leave school and run away. She's just too black-and-white. Too much of a stickler for rules. Please, can you get that Amber Alert issued?" With a fresh slew of tears, she included both detectives in her plea-filled glance.

"We're working on it," Jeanine Crosby said. "We've just got a few more questions for you if you're okay to answer them."

"Of course I'm okay. Whatever it takes."

They asked again about Hope's friends. About anyone who gave Amanda any cause for concern. Her answers were identical to the first time they'd questioned her.

But Hope at that park… Was there any reason that didn't involve abduction and horror that her daughter could have been over there?

"She knows kids that I don't know," she said. "Kids she talks to in class that she doesn't hang out with outside of school. I've heard her talk about a Mary. And a Shelby. One of them, Shelby, I think, doesn't have a great home life. Hope didn't know for sure, but thought maybe Shelby's dad had a drinking problem. Anyway, if she was in some kind of trouble, Shelby, I mean, or really anyone she might have heard about, who needed immediate assistance, I could see Hope going to do what she could…"

Amanda had taught her daughter to be aware of the suffering of others. To do for others, instead of always expecting to be done for.

Oh, God. Had the lessons from Amanda's own journey through life, her own issues, steered her child right into danger?

"When was the last time either of you saw your parents?" Detective Wedbush asked. His tone had changed.

Amanda looked straight at him. "Three weeks ago. On Sunday." She named the hour. "You can check the visitor logs to see every time we've been there. It's all digitized." They'd know that. She said it anyway.

"Have you been in contact with them other than those times?"

"My father, no. My mom writes to us, and when she does, we respond. And there will be records of those letters, too." Nothing went in or out of the state prison without them. Shuddering away a sob as she took a deep breath, she added, "I have nothing to hide. Ask whatever you want. Look wherever you want. Just, please, don't waste time looking at me that's going to take away from the focus of finding Hope. I can't guarantee you that my parents didn't get to her somehow. As you know, Hudson found that bank routing information on her computer. But I'm telling you that if they did, she didn't know what they were doing. And I had no knowledge of it, either. And if they did…" Her voice broke and she sat up straighter to finish with a wobblier tone, "We need that Amber Alert."

She'd made a terrible mistake. She never should have taken Hope to meet her parents. If she was responsible for her sweet girl being hurt, she was never ever going to forgive herself.

But this wasn't about her. It was about doing whatever she could to help everyone else do their jobs: to find her daughter.

Not wasting their focus on sympathy for her. She sniffed. Dried her eyes.

She sensed Hudson's presence before she actually realized she'd heard him come down the hall.

And the scent of him. He couldn't be using the same soap or deodorant he'd used as a teenager taking whatever was given to him at the children's home. Yet her brain insisted his scent was familiar.

She didn't turn to look at him. She didn't want him seeing any residual neediness in her gaze, but she didn't know how not to need him. Not back then, and especially not in the current moment. He was the miracle worker in the room. Testimonials on the Sierra's Web website even said so.

"There's no sign of anything on Amanda's computer." He was standing behind her as he addressed the detectives. "Not that I've seen at a first glance," he added. "Nothing on any sector searches. And for what it's worth, I believe she has nothing to do with this. What I'm finding on Hope's computer, it's jagged, good, but amateurish. Computer techies all have their own signatures. This kid has one…"

He almost sounded impressed. But extremely serious, too, giving Amanda the sense that Hudson believed Hope was in trouble.

Not that she'd run away, or that she was working some grand scheme with her grandmother.

"I'm not done by a long shot, but heard your voices and was hoping you brought the cell phone."

Wedbush reached into his pocket, pulled out the smartphone and handed it to Hudson.

Just seeing them there…emotion swamped her again. Gratitude. Warmth. Longing. With the ever-present panic-laced fear for Hope's safety. It was overwhelming and…

She stood. "I have to go to the park," she said. "I need

to be where she was. Maybe I'll see something no one else would recognize." Maybe she'd smell her daughter's rose-scented bath gel.

"I don't advise that you go anywhere," Crosby said as she and Wedbush stood as well. "And most definitely not to the park right now. We've got dogs there and people going over every inch of the place…"

Relief was a blessing for the blip it lasted. They were looking. Calling in the dogs. Doing far more than she could.

And with that, she had to do what was turning out to be the hardest thing of all.

Waiting while others searched for her heart and soul.

She'd made her lists. Delivered them via email to the detectives before she'd even given them to Hudson.

She'd called Hudson.

Now she had to stay out of everyone's way.

"I want to go see my parents," she said then. "I'll record the meetings. Whatever you need. But if they know something, my mother will tell me. If she knows Hope's missing."

"We've already had a team of detectives there. They both were pretty convincing in their shock, concern and lack of knowledge."

But detectives were outsiders. Amanda had learned long ago how that worked. "I'm their daughter," she said aloud. "I won't go if you think it will hurt the investigation, but if you don't, then I have to try."

"I'll go with her," Hudson offered. "I have specific tracking questions I'd like to ask."

His company had a stellar reputation for working on crimes all across the nation. He was only doing his job.

So why was Amanda suddenly feeling like his offer to accompany her had been personal?

To help her get what she needed?

It was a question she wouldn't entertain.

Or allow herself to answer.

Chapter 5

Hudson dumped the contents of Hope's entire hard drive to a cleared laptop that traveled with him for just that purpose. Turning on his hot spot, he spent the forty-five-minute drive down to the prison complex doing what he'd been doing most of the morning, scrolling through screen after screen of code.

Finding back doors into things that had no reason to be hidden in the first place, looking for what Hope might have needed to hide. It could be that she'd been learning and playing around with encryption just as a hobby.

He had to find out. His window to find the girl still alive dwindled with every hour that passed.

His hunch told him she'd had a specific purpose. The timing was suspicious, for one. Everything had started shortly after she'd visited her grandparents for the first time.

And that banking number. He'd recognized the routing number because he'd dealt with it on another case—a federal case. But on Hope's computer it hadn't appeared in any format or with anything else that led him to believe that the girl had known what it meant. He'd traced it to a text message sent to her email address through a third-party app. She'd deleted the email without responding, but it looked like she'd opened it. His thought was that whoever had sent it had had the number embedded on her computer, which told him that the account number was there, too. Finding the sender was proving more difficult.

And until he found the sender, he really had nothing to say. He'd found a routing number to a foreign bank. It could have been a spam message that she'd clicked on, and nothing more.

"My mom and dad… I used to talk about you all the time…and…Hudson is an unusual name."

"Okay." He didn't want to think about those long-ago days she'd spoken to them about him. Though he'd never met them, he'd hated her parents back then for what they'd done to her. Hated that they made her see them. Hated how broken she'd been each time she'd returned. Which was why he'd been there waiting. Every single time.

No one else had been.

"Just wanted you prepared. In case they ask if you're the same guy."

He wondered how many guys there'd been in the past nearly fifteen years. Would have been a hell of a lot happier if he didn't care. "Did they ever meet Hope's dad?"

"No." That was pretty succinct.

"I told them he was a one-night thing and left it at that," she added when he remained silent. So that's what happened. That made him feel things. Sad for her, but kind of vindicated. He had to admit that he was glad she hadn't just gone right out and replaced him within months of his leaving.

Lord knew he'd mourned her for much longer than that—though there was only one person he'd ever mentioned her to. His friend Sierra.

He'd always thought that Sierra and Amanda would have liked each other. They'd both been emotionally sensitive and wicked smart.

He couldn't start thinking about Sierra now, though. He had a job to do—one that Amanda was desperately waiting for him to do.

And there wasn't much for them to say to each other. Anything would be too much…more than he wanted to get into.

And probably more than *she* could handle.

He studied the screen. Brought up a couple of other windows. And then one more. He needed to ask which of her friends would have had access to her computer, just so he could verify that what he found wasn't suspicious to avoid wasting time following it any further.

Amanda had pulled into a driveway, followed it around and stopped in a spot as though it was her own. It probably felt that way to her, considering all the years she'd visited there.

"You chose to keep coming here even after you were no longer being forced to do so." The courts had agreed, as part of her parents' plea agreement, to grant them visitation rights until Amanda graduated high school.

The night she and Hudson had made love for the first time, on her eighteenth birthday, had been the last time she'd had to see them.

He was focused on the scene before them, but those weren't the words he'd been planning to say. He'd just found something—some curious activity on Hope's hard drive. Either she'd posed as someone else, she'd let someone else use her computer or she'd been hacked. There'd been a different sign-in and password used in a few places. He didn't know the program or app yet.

Yet.

"They're my parents," she was saying, her face strangely calm, and somewhat vacant as she turned off the engine. "They're the only family I have."

"There was that uncle, your mother's brother. And he had a son." Why was he pressing the point? He was there to try to help save a life, not delve into a lifelong past.

"I've never met either one of them," she said. "They don't count."

He remembered them very clearly. When she'd first come to the home, she'd clung to the belief that they'd come forward, take her in. But her mother had shunned her blue-collar family when she'd married George Smythe. And when they'd turned out to be crooks, there was such an angry mob, the shunned maternal family hadn't wanted anything to do with them.

No one had.

Amanda hadn't blamed them.

But Hudson had. She'd been fourteen. An innocent, hurting kid. She shouldn't have been made to pay for things her folks had done.

And yet she'd paid.

Over and over again.

And as they entered the cold, unadorned building, Hudson hoped to God that she wasn't being made to pay again.

With Hope's life.

They saw her father first. She always did. She had to get through the less pleasant experience, so she could get to the easier one. End with the easier one. Go back out to life with her mother's love ringing last, and therefore loudest, in her ears.

Checking in, which included submitting to a search and walking down to the visitor's room, felt completely surreal. She'd been through the process so many times she barely acknowledged it happening. And yet…this time was all new. All of the times she'd imagined Hudson there with her, making that walk down that very same dingy hallway, it had never been with her daughter missing and him as a virtual stranger.

When she'd been in high school, she'd had him with her, in spirit, every single time she'd been to the prison. Had imagined him walking beside her as her husband. Her soul mate.

Someone who would never betray her, leave her, as her parents had done.

Her mind kept telling her the current day couldn't be happening. That she was going to wake up from the debilitating nightmare to find Hope safely in her room.

And Hudson across town and completely out of her life.

Starting to shake with nerves, with tension, she

grasped for something else upon which to focus. "Why did you come back to Arizona?"

She'd been shocked years before, when she'd done a search on him and found that he'd returned home. It was the last thing she'd expected.

They'd reached the door of the room, and as they waited for the guard to let them in, she looked up at Hudson. The safe distance between them was surreal, too. In the past, even before they were a couple, he'd always stayed so close to her.

"Everyone wanted to have the home office someplace warm and fun to visit, and we decided that it should be located close to me because our IT capabilities were essential in order to work all over the country like we do. We tap into a lot of databases that are available to all of us." His shrug sent her flying back a lot of years, to a memory of her head on that shoulder. A less filled-out version of it. "I came back after college. Arizona's home to me," he added. "And Lord knows home is a nebulous enough thing in my life without changing it up yet again."

She accepted his answer. And the silly disappointment that had accompanied it. She'd known that he hadn't come back to be close to her. There'd been no valid cause to take personal comfort from his nearness in the ensuing years since he'd returned.

The door opened, and thoughts of the past fled as she once again faced stark, cold reality. Head high, shoulders back and step confident, she went in to try to get even a smidgeon of truth out of her father's verbose and friendly conversation.

For Hope, she'd do far worse. Walk on hot coals. Call

the love of her life for help and pretend he was just an IT expert.

For Hope, she'd do whatever it took.

Hudson disliked Amanda's father on sight. No big surprise there. He'd walked into the room loaded with memories of trying to comfort the distraught child George Smythe had left behind.

He could barely bring himself to take the hand the orange-suited man held out. He didn't appreciate the firmness of the older man's grasp. And most particularly, he bristled at the way the man took ownership of Amanda, thanking Hudson for being such a good friend to his daughter those many years ago.

Most of all, he resented the fact that the man just continued to run the show, not even acknowledging the reason for the unscheduled visit, though he most definitely knew about Hope's disappearance. Detectives had been to see him that morning.

George seemed to take the attention as his due. Owning the world around him.

"We're not here to socialize, Dad," Amanda cut him off thirty seconds into the visit. Hudson, who'd just taken a breath to cut the man off himself, took a mental step back instead.

"The police think that Hope's disappearance could have something to do with you and Mom. I need to know if there's anything…anything…that could put Hope's life in danger."

"No." His answer was quick. Strongly uttered. He was frowning. Shaking his head. Dropped down to the bench on his side of the table. When Amanda didn't follow suit, didn't sit, Hudson remained standing beside her.

"There's a routing number on her computer," he said. He inserted enough technical jargon into his rhetoric to show George that Hudson was the pro here, then asked a couple of pertinent questions about dark web money laundering.

The only satisfaction he got out of the three minutes they were in that room was the deflation of the man's pompous attitude.

Lifting his chin as he answered each question, Amanda's father swore that he knew nothing, had said nothing to Hope, and nothing to anyone else regarding Hope or anything to do with her. He swore that he'd turned over every single bank account, every dime he'd swindled, as part of the plea agreement, adding that he'd done it to spare his daughter a long, drawn-out court battle. And to ensure his visitation rights with her.

What he didn't do was offer Amanda any condolence or offer of hope as they left. Not even an *I hope you find her.*

The lack of compassion ate at Hudson. But whether it was because it meant George knew more than he'd let on, or just because Amanda had been cursed with such an ass as a father, he wasn't sure.

Amanda was prepared for her mother. The second the woman entered the visitor's room, in her orange top and elastic-waist-banded off-color orange pants, Amanda started to shake. Patricia was crying and reached to hug Amanda over the table separating them.

Submitting as much because she needed things from

her mother quickly as anything else, Amanda sat, dry-eyed, and said, "Dad knows something."

Patricia looked down. She fiddled with a scratch on the table, rubbing it. And pinching at a roughed edge. She glanced at Hudson, but Amanda didn't introduce him. She'd intended to. But after the visit with her father—she just couldn't.

Hudson didn't belong there as her friend. Or whatever he'd once been to her. He was there as an IT expert who had questions.

"You have to tell me, Mom. No matter what it is." The statement brooked zero argument.

And got none. Patricia, unlike her husband, had taken responsibility for her actions from the very beginning. The only thing she'd asked in return was to see Amanda.

It was for her mother, not her father, that Amanda continued to visit the prison every single month.

"You know something. And now Hope is in danger." *And how could you do that? How could you put your own granddaughter in danger? How could you not tell me?* The words screamed inside her, dying to get out.

"I found a routing number on her computer." Hudson's voice came from beside her. He was sitting close enough that she could feel his heat against the side of her thigh, her shoulder. Amanda noticed. But couldn't let herself succumb to its comfort. She studied, instead, the deepening lines on her once beautiful mother's face. Made more pronounced by the sudden frown encapsulating the grief and worry with which she'd entered the room.

Hudson had seen pictures of both her parents. Seen

pictures of her living life big prior to coming to the home. After nearly two decades in prison, her parents were hardly recognizable to those old likenesses. She hoped she didn't resemble the spoiled little princess she'd been back then, either.

As with her father, Hudson asked for any information regarding the foreign bank in question. Had the two of them done any business with the bank at any time for any reason? He asked for details of business transactions that made no sense to her, including ways they'd conducted transactions. He probed technical routes they'd taken to make trailing money almost impossible.

It made Amanda's head spin. He fired off a series of inquiries to which Patricia just kept shaking her head and giving the exact response George had. "No." Again and again. Mixed with an original, "I don't know, George handled that," a time or two.

They'd spent over an hour of precious time and gotten nowhere.

"Mom," she said, leaning forward, talking in a near whisper though no one but the guard at the door across the room was present, other than the three of them. "I need you tell me if there are any secrets I don't know about. Anything that you and Dad have been hiding. Because this is the only thing that makes sense. Hope just isn't into anything nefarious. And that routing number showed up on her computer after visiting you. Did you somehow pass her some information without my knowing? Maybe even without her knowing? You've got to tell me the truth. Or I swear to you, I'll never be back to see you again."

Patricia's eyes welled with tears, her hair so unimpressive with the short straight strands hanging around her face. "I gave her nothing," she said softly. "I would never, ever do anything to put either of you in danger."

"Not even to protect Dad? Or to protect yourself from whatever you think he could do?"

She'd long ago figured out that while her mother had been knowingly complicit in what the couple had done, she'd also been intimidated by her father. Because no way could Amanda believe that something as pure and good as love could have made her such a supporter of the man.

Money could have, though. And greed.

"I know Dad was lying to us, Mom. He lifted his chin when Hudson mentioned the routing number from that bank." She'd figured out several years before that that chin lift was a tell. Maybe she'd always known, had always barricaded her heart when he got that look on his face, but she'd really realized that it meant deceit the day he'd told her that he'd die for her, he loved her so much.

He'd been trying to get her to write letters to the governor and other key people, asking them to speak on the Smythes' behalf to the parole board. And in that instant, she'd just known.

He always lifts his chin like that when he lies.

"Hudson?" Patricia said, her gaze sharpening as she glanced at the man Amanda had decided not to introduce.

Damn. She'd purposely planned to avoid...

"Mom. Don't change the subject. There's a bank account, isn't there?" The lead in her gut told her there was.

And that somehow it had something to do with Hope's disappearance.

"Are you the same Hudson who was such a good friend to my Amanda years ago?"

No mention of the children's home. Or the court case that had put Amanda there. And no way could she let her mother off the hook.

"Mom, the bank account."

"What bank account?" Patricia's watery blue gaze, faded from years of incarceration, turned back to her.

"Hope's missing, Mom," she reiterated, biting the words out through gritted teeth. "Her life is in danger." There was warning in her tone, but desperation, too. Moving toward begging.

The police were out there. Hopefully finding her daughter. But if her mother could help…

If there was some detail that could help narrow or focus Hudson's search of hours' and hours' worth of information yet to be deciphered from Hope's computer…

"There is an offshore account."

Amanda wasn't even sure she'd heard the words, though her mother was no longer whispering. She'd made the pronouncement in a normal tone. As though, once she'd decided to admit the truth, she had nothing left to hide.

"I need the information," Hudson said, taking out his phone, opening an app, and finger-typing in rapid succession as her mom listed off a series of numbers.

Amanda, in total shock, in spite of what her gut had been telling her, sat there, mouth open, watching the woman who'd given birth to her. Watching her finally tell the truth, after years of swearing she'd confessed all.

Amanda's mind had doubted her mother. But her heart…

Was apparently a very slow learner. But she was catching on.

And Patricia Smythe had better hope that it wasn't too little too late.

"Who else knows about this account?" Hudson asked what Amanda should have been thinking about finding out.

"No one." Patricia spoke directly to him. "Just George and me."

Standing abruptly, Amanda waited while Hudson put his phone back in his pocket. She glanced at her mother, caught her gaze and held on. One heart to another speaking silently of a betrayal from which there'd be no coming back.

What have my parents done? And how is Hope caught in the middle?

"It was for you," her mother said, sounding more like herself than she had in a long time. "We'll get out before we die," she continued. "We were going to settle in Morocco. Take you and Hope with us. And give you back the good life. We were going to make it all up to you."

"You still don't get it, do you?" Amanda asked, stepping back as Patricia stood, too. "That life…the money that rules it…it's not good, Mom. I don't want any part of it. The good life is what I share with my daughter…"

Her voice broke, and she turned away. She couldn't get to the door fast enough.

Through it.

Down the hall and out.

Stumbling into the bright Arizona sunshine, it was like she was fourteen again. Overwhelmed. Unable to see clearly. Delirious with hurt. Fear.

Needing Hudson to ease the pain.

She couldn't fall into his arms and find solace as she had all those years ago.

But at least, for the moment, he was there.

For the moment, it was enough.

Chapter 6

Hudson offered to drive. He was only moderately surprised when Amanda said she was fine and would rather have him working. He was more than a bit relieved, too. Truth was, he'd rather be buried in his computer than dealing with the emotions swirling out of her at the moment.

He couldn't take her in his arms, and he didn't know of any other way to help. No words were going to ease her suffering or make her any less alone.

"I have to call Crosby and Wedbush," he said as soon as he was buckled in his seat.

"I know."

She'd buckled in and was starting the car. Her hand moved to the gear shift between them, moving to put the small luxury SUV into Drive, but he stopped her, covering her hand with his own. He recognized the mistake the second he'd done it. Touching of any kind was absolutely out.

And there he was, his palm covering the back of her hand. Cradling it. She glanced toward their hands. Didn't pull away. Just swallowed hard.

Stared out the front windshield.

"One of my parents told her about the bank account," she said. "Either that or Mom was lying about no one else knowing, and I tend to believe it's the former. No way my daughter just dreamed up that routing number and typed it on her computer."

She spoke calmly. Without emotion.

A lie to the woman inside her.

But he understood. She was dealing with liars.

Who also happened to be the people who'd given her life.

She had to protect herself.

"Was she ever alone with either one of them?" She'd said she'd always been present for Hope's visits, and he'd been wondering how either of her grandparents could have slipped her dangerous information without Amanda knowing about it.

"No." She shook her head. Then frowned. "Maybe. I wasn't always as vigilant with my mom when we visited. I went to the bathroom once. We'd had fast food on the way to the prison, and something didn't sit well with me. And I talked to the guard sometimes, but right there, watching them the whole time… I worried about Mom, and left her talking with Hope at the table so I could check with the guard and make sure Mom was okay…"

Her voice broke, and he saw the tremble in her chin as she said, "Oh, God, I did this. It's my fault…"

"It's not your fault." He said the words, knowing them to be utter truth. And recognizing that she wasn't going to believe them. Of course she was blaming herself. In a lot of ways, she was Hope's sole protector.

He'd once felt like he was Amanda's. Knew firsthand the emotional toll such a job carried.

"I'm sorry." It wasn't anywhere close to enough. And all he had. He held her gaze as she turned to him. Wishing he had more to give her.

Wishing…he didn't know what. Maybe that he'd been who she'd needed him to be.

"I'm glad you called me," he added. Saw the small break in her lips, the almost-smile, before she faced forward and those soft lips hardened into a thin line again. He let go of her hand, and she put the car in gear.

"There are other options." Hudson had been off the phone for several minutes. Was already deeply into code on the computer screen, but couldn't get away from the idea that the silence had to be excruciating for her. The Amanda he knew dealt with tragedy by talking about it.

To me.

"It could be that one of your parents gave Hope's email address to someone else who knows about the account. Could be that someone hacked into her computer, embedded something that would make it look like Hope was accessing that money…"

The girl's encryption practices were bothering him. They implied that she had something to hide. Unless she was just fascinated with computers and had been learning skills. He could relate to that.

Amanda would have heard him on the phone, telling Steven Wedbush about the foreign username and password sign-in that he'd found just before they'd gone into the prison. She hadn't asked about any of the conversation, though, as he'd hung up.

And he'd left her to her processing. He was her computer expert. Not her confidant. It was all he could be. Allowing her to think there could be more was just wrong.

No matter how pulled he was in a different direction.

It was only the moment. Old habits died hard.

And he knew where those led him, too. Running for the hills.

"We don't even know if the money's been accessed," she said. "Or how much was there to begin with."

That was the detectives' job to find out and deal with. It was pretty clear Amanda didn't give a damn about the account, any funds, one way or another.

That was still sitting in his mental *new information needing to be processed* inbox. She'd immediately told her mother that a privileged life wasn't the good life. But in all the years he'd known her as teenagers, she'd lamented exactly the opposite.

She'd been focused on a future of living the good life again. Doing it honestly—but doing it.

It had been a life an orphaned kid with no prospects like him couldn't possibly have provided for her. He'd seen the writing on the wall from the very beginning of their friendship.

He'd always figured she had, too. Which had made

everything that much more difficult when they'd become a couple...so much harder to deal with...so much more pressure on him...

Nope. Wrong road. U-turn.

What has changed for Amanda?

"I'm doing everything I can to figure out Hope's involvement, if any," he said, focusing back on the screen in front of him. "I've got a team of people who freelance for me." He had to keep his mind completely and irrevocably on the job. "With your permission, I'd like to call someone to help scour every file. He'll work remotely. I'll still be looking as well, and will lead the work. But because of the passing time, I'd like extra eyes on this."

"I want you to do whatever it takes." She'd stopped at a light and turned to look at him. He could see her in his peripheral vision. Could feel that gaze. He pretended absolute focus on the screen.

"And I'm glad I called you, too."

His heart blipped.

He had to wonder there for a second if he was as smart a man as he thought he was.

The forensic team was just leaving as they got back to the house. While Hudson returned to computer searching, she made a couple of sandwiches for a late lunch. Not sure she could take a bite, but she'd told him she'd feed him. He'd always loved grilled cheese sandwiches with mayonnaise, made with shredded cheddar, and, through him, she'd learned to love them, too.

Hope had grown up on them.

Though he barely acknowledged her presence when she brought the sandwich to him in her office, where he'd moved Hope's computer, his laptop and Amanda's computer positioned in the middle of her much larger desk, she felt more capable, just seeing him there.

As though his existence gave her strength.

At fourteen that had been understandable. At thirty-two, not so much.

Right now, she had absolutely no wherewithal to analyze any of it. She couldn't care about her inappropriate feelings for her first love, who was now her only hope to find her daughter.

How was he going to react when she dropped the bombshell she was holding?

And she couldn't process how her mother had been lying to her all of the years she'd been visiting her. Believing in her.

I just need Hope home.

And as the seconds ticked by, moving into minutes and then an hour, with no word, it took everything she had to maintain some sense of equilibrium. She paced. Wiped counters that were already spotless. Cleaned windows—mostly so she could stand there and look out them. She couldn't work. Couldn't watch television. Could hardly focus as the time for the school day to be done moved irrevocably closer.

Would Hope just come home, pretending that it had been a typical school day? Unaware that her absence had been noticed to the point of police all over the city knowing about it?

She hung on to the possibility—even as she knew the chance was slim to none—that her daughter would think she could cut school and have no one know. Even her mother.

Which didn't mean that Hope wouldn't come home after school with a damned good explanation as to why she'd done what she did.

The fact that Hope had left on her own kept playing with her. Sometimes, her panic eased with the thought that Hope was in control of whatever was happening. That she wasn't a victim.

Sometimes, it scared her even more. What on earth would cause Hope to knowingly break all the rules? Act totally out of character?

And worry everyone?

For all the solitariness of those early-afternoon hours, everything changed in minutes after school let out.

Mothers of Hope's friends started calling. As the word spread, her phone was dinging missed calls constantly. She took one or two of them, attempted to have a conversation, but ended up just letting most go to voice mail.

She took Jeanine Crosby's call, though.

An official Amber Alert had been released.

And Hope still didn't come home.

Hudson knew the time. He heard Amanda's phone ringing. Just as he'd been aware of her every second that they'd been home. Could hear spraying. Hear her walking. Hear her in the kitchen. In the living room, even though she was around the corner and down the hall from the room he was in. It was as though his senses were heightened when she was around.

Another familiar flashback.

Others hadn't seemed to be aware of the acuteness

of her suffering, but he'd been unable to escape the awareness. He'd felt her as though she was a part of him.

But no more.

He wasn't at all surprised at the sandwich she'd delivered, made just how he liked it. He had almost gotten up to follow her out and make certain she was eating, too.

But turned to the computer screen instead as he ate. He had his best guy scouring the same data. Between the two of them, they had to find more than curious anomalies. There had to be something there that was going to lead them to the girl. The fact that there'd been no ransom call was not good.

He didn't know whether or not Crosby or Wedbush had talked to Amanda about that. About the fact that if the kidnappers didn't call, it more than likely meant that Hope wasn't going to be returned. It meant that what they needed they could get just from Hope. And when they no longer needed her...

As he'd been sifting through emails, account posts, as well as coding, he'd begun to get a sense of the girl Amanda was raising.

Hope was smart. And savvy. As far as he could tell, she didn't put anything out on social media that could put her at risk. Mostly she posted about tennis.

Articles. Stats. Workouts. Matches and competitions. Both professional and her own amateur stuff.

By late afternoon he felt as though he'd met most of her friends. Had a sense of personalities. And also carried a sense, growing stronger by the second, that he needed to check on Amanda.

He messaged John Badger, the associate he'd called in to help him on his own dime, that he was stepping away from the computer for a second. He told him to direct all communication to his cell phone, then went in search of the distraught mother.

The client who'd called him to help find her missing daughter.

He could give her an update. They'd found a name in some coding, with a message attached, from a girl who wasn't in any of Hope's contacts, her social media accounts' friends lists or her high school roster.

The news would do nothing but make her lose hope that they were going to find anything that could help them. The message had been completely innocuous. An epistle about cool ways to wear ponytails. All split up by code.

The only thing remarkable about it all was that he hadn't been able to trace the code back to a messaging app of any kind.

He'd put John on it. And put more pressure on himself. Finding the bank routing number early on, he'd been hopeful he could wrap the job up quickly.

Get Amanda's daughter back to her quickly.

Ease everyone's pain.

And go back home.

Instead, there he was, going out to find his client—Amanda—with nothing to offer her. Nothing to do with finding her daughter, at any rate.

She spun from the window when she heard him enter the living room, an almost wild expression on her face. "I can't just stay here, doing nothing, Hud," she said, frantic-sounding. "I'm going to lose my mind just standing here doing nothing. It's clear she's not coming right home. My next-door neighbor…she called a bit ago, when she heard the news...she offered to come over and sit at the house. Mabel's been helping me keep an eye on Hope since we moved here a few years ago. And...I have to go... I've got my cell phone. And standing here..." Wringing her hands, she shook her head and swept out of the room, into the kitchen, where she grabbed her purse and keys.

"Hey." He went after her. Knowing that he couldn't just let her take off like that. She shouldn't be out alone. She should be home in case any news of Hope turned up.

The look she gave him stopped any of those things from following the lone "hey" out of his mouth. Instead, he surprised himself with, "Can I come along?"

He needed a break from staring at the screen. John had fresh eyes and was every bit as detail-oriented and skilled as Hudson was, which was why he was on the Sierra's Web list of contracted experts.

"I'm fine," she said over her shoulder, making a beeline for the door. Hudson caught her just with her hand on the knob. Covering it, his body half leaning over hers, his face inches from the delicate features that had been forever emblazoned on his memory.

"You're not fine," he told her. "You're handling all of this remarkably well, but no way you could possibly expect to be fine right now." Words just sprang forth. There was no time for judgment or thoughts about who he was and wasn't. "You shouldn't be gone long, but I understand you needing to get out. I need a break from the screen or I'm going to miss something, and I'd like to ask some questions about Hope. I've had my initial look with a fresh perspective. Now I'd like to know more about her in case it can lead me to what I haven't found. May I please come with you?"

She stared at him, her mouth slightly open.

And then nodded.

"We should wait for Mabel," he said quickly, hoping to cash in on her momentary complacency. They'd been gone earlier, but with the forensic team in residence.

"She's on her way over," Amanda said. "And she has a key."

"I'd like to drive." She'd left her car in her driveway, but his was out front. "If she does happen to make her way back and is in some kind of trouble, it might be good for her to see your car here." The reasoning came to him on the fly.

But it worked. Amanda nodded, and he pulled his keys from his pocket.

He wasn't being a friend. He was just a pro doing his job.

Or so he told himself as he followed her out the door.

Chapter 7

"I was afraid people were going to begin stopping by," Amanda said quietly. They were in Hudson's car, seat belts on, but had yet to pull away from the house. "I know they're well-meaning, but I can't deal with sympathy right now. I'm afraid I'd break. I need to go to the park behind the high school." The park where Hope's lone shoe was found. Before he could argue, she added, "When I found out I was pregnant with Hope, I knew I was going to do it alone, and though I was scared out of my wits, I read this thing about a mother's intuition…" She broke off for a second, her scattered mind zoning over to her mother for a moment. She viscerally felt the pain of Patricia's ultimate betrayal—a hidden bank account that denoted a continuation of the lies, deceit and conscienceless illegalities that had ruined all of their lives.

Once she'd gotten pregnant with Hope, she'd seen her mother in a new light. She'd seen a mother who loved her child unconditionally and only wanted what was best for her. One she wouldn't ever deceive.

A wrong light.

She pushed the pang away and watched as Hudson pulled up to a stop sign at the end of their street and turned toward the gate that would take them out of her community. "I believed that a mother really did get a special gift of intuition when she gave birth, and if I always listened to my intuition, Hope and I would be okay." So had Patricia not listened? Or had Amanda's ideas about intuition been a fairy tale she'd told herself?

A make-believe on which she'd built a life.

She was so confused. So lost...

But Hudson was there. And she absolutely couldn't turn to him. "My intuition is telling me to go to the park," she said. And so she would go. No matter what.

"I just have to be where she was." Maybe it wasn't intuition at all, but rather a selfish need to be close to Hope's last known whereabouts. To see for herself that the park was calm, with no sign of struggle or tragedy.

So that she could find the faith to hold on.

To believe that all would be well. She couldn't give up on that thought. Hope needed her to keep believing.

"You were so young..." Hudson's voice broke into her thoughts, a rendition of what she'd been hearing from him all day—but with more. He sounded more like the young man in her memory. As though he was a personal friend.

She knew he wasn't. Knew, too, that he might hate her when Hope was back and he found out that she'd robbed him of his daughter's childhood. But for the moment, she let herself be the girl who'd been his friend.

Before they'd become more than friends. And then not *even* friends.

Looking around, keeping her eyes peeled for any sign of her daughter, she said, "I didn't feel young." Having had her childhood stripped away at fourteen, by eighteen she'd been so certain she'd reached full maturity.

"It was a lot to take on all alone. Did you ever consider giving her up for adoption?"

The conversation was in dangerous territory, but she didn't fight it. She had to tell him. "No," she said, knowing then that if he asked about Hope's father, she was going to be completely honest with him.

"That was partially why I didn't tell the father," she said slowly, needing him to know, to hear with an open mind, before the rest of the truth clouded his ability to understand. "He would have wanted me to either get an abortion or give her up for adoption, and I knew, the second I realized I was pregnant, that I had to have her. That I'd been given the chance to have a family of my own. But that I had to step up to the challenge, to not be the self-centered person you saw me to be—which was largely correct, by the way—but to be someone who not only took care of herself, but who also thought of others, who tended to others, instead of focusing on her own pain or happiness." Trees passed slowly, neighborhoods, corners, trash bins and buildings. An alley.

All with no sign of Hope. Or even a sight of a teenager with long blond hair.

"I had no right to say those things to you." His tone

had changed again and was becoming more distant. Part of her was relieved.

"You were right in your assessment," she acknowledged. Maybe he'd been too blunt. But that didn't much matter anymore.

And then telling herself to let it go, she looked at the near-stranger beside her and said, "There was no way I could have had an abortion, or have given her up. And alone like I was, it took everything I had to provide for myself and my growing baby. I couldn't get into it with the father, too. Or have him pressuring me."

"I'm not judging you, Manda." His pet name for her, the way he'd said it, brought a fresh spate of tears to the surface. "From everything I've seen today, you've done a wonderful job with her. You're a great mom and clearly love her dearly."

He didn't know he was the father she'd chosen to keep in the dark. And still, his words of praise warmed her.

"Clearly you made a good choice, keeping her."

Was it clear? Even with her missing? Had she somehow led her baby girl into danger? By giving her contact with her grandparents, not teaching her well enough how to keep herself safe, or by missing some key sign that should have let her see that Hope was struggling somehow?

Truth was, Hudson was probably just trying his best to make her feel better in an untenable situation—not passing words of substance regarding her life choices.

When he knew the truth, he might have an entirely different message to deliver on the subject.

For the moment, she had to stay strong. To quit dithering about things she couldn't change and find a way to change the one thing that mattered—her daughter being absent.

He asked some questions about Hope's interest in tennis, including a particular tournament she'd played in during the winter break. He was curious about Hope's interest in computers, too, and wanted to know if she'd had any formal training.

When he was searching Hope's computer, Amanda wanted to tell Hudson that she'd shown a propensity for technical awareness from the time she was a toddler. She'd always been taking things apart and putting them back together again. She'd chosen computer science electives at school, too. Amanda had long ago determined that Hope was going to follow in her father's footsteps in terms of mastering the technical arena.

But her father didn't know that. Not yet.

They'd arrived at the park. She had her belt off and door opened before Hudson had his keys out of the ignition.

They weren't the only ones around, of course. February weather in Arizona was perfect for park days, unlike the one-hundred-fifteen-degree temperatures of summer that left the parks mostly deserted as everyone stayed inside where it was cool.

Amanda was overdressed, too, in the black business clothes with which she'd started what was supposed to have been a normal workday. Nothing stopped her or distracted her concentration as she walked every yard of that park, starting with the tennis and basketball courts and then to the small brick bathrooms, two stalls each for women and men. She headed from one to the other, but before she'd charged into the men's room, Hudson stopped her. He'd get that one.

Ten minutes into her forage, she slowed, realizing that she was looking for a needle in a haystack.

"We can ask if anyone has seen her," Hudson suggested.

Until then, she'd barely seen the people milling around, other than to find them an irritant if they were in her way. There were a couple of guys on the basketball court. A teenager sitting on a swing, as though waiting for someone. A pickup football game with players ranging from junior high to near-adults.

And a couple of girls, a bit older than Hope, lounging at a splintering gray picnic table. She headed in that direction. Trying not to notice the bus stop not far off from them. If Hope had been taken and hauled onto that bus…or had run through the park to catch the bus…

Neither scenario was a good one.

Both were extremely feasible.

Neither of the girls at the table had seen anyone looking like the picture of Hope Amanda showed them on her phone. Not that they seemed to be paying attention to anything but themselves.

"I don't think they would have noticed if she'd been sitting at the table with them," Hudson said as they walked away, trying to make her feel better.

Thing was, it worked. Just having him there, having her back, was working a kind of magic on her. He was refilling the well of hope and faith that had been dangerously dwindling at the house.

"Crosby told me that they found the shoe in a wash behind an orange tree," Hudson was saying, looking ahead in the distance. "Looks like that's the only orange tree around here," he added.

She walked side by side with him with hurried steps, moving quickly toward that one fruit tree, and the two-foot-wide dip just beyond designed to drain water from the park during the monsoons. February was fruit-bearing time, but when they reached it, the tree was completely barren. But the dirt…was it extra mussed?

"Does it look to you like there was a scuffle here?" she asked, referring to the hard desert ground not far from the tree. He studied the spot, then shrugged.

A polite way of telling her she was seeing things that weren't there?

He didn't appear to be just biding time, though. He was walking the area, head bent, as though looking for a stripe of gold in the mineral-laden Arizona ground. She scuffed a gum wrapper with the toe of her pump. Stretched her line of investigation further, following the drain gulley—a strip that held the greenest and healthiest grass since it was also the area that got the most water, thinking that she'd somehow recognize that Hope had been there, know which direction she'd gone. Or feel some of what she'd been feeling?

She had to know if her little girl had been scared there that morning. In fear for her life?

Running from something? To something?

A torn piece of paper in the grass caught her eye. She went toward it, knowing she was being ridiculous, out there looking for clues as though the professionals who'd scoured the park before her wouldn't have already found anything that might have been there. And, just like the gum wrapper, the few rocks that had glistened as though more than just stone, she made sure the paper was just a scrap torn from some kid's notebook. Or a wrapper for something. She kicked it with her shoe. Flipping it up enough that she got a better look.

Her heart started to pound for a second when she recognized that she'd scuffed up a partial photo. Squatting down, she looked closer. The rendition was grainy. A thumbnail-size printout on regular copy paper. And not even the whole picture. The picture had ripped, leaving eyes and a nose and part of a chin, and part of a name, too.

Almost as though it had been ripped in half.

Or ripped off a page from someone's schoolbook as they'd been roughhousing in the park on the way home from school.

"You find something?" Hudson was beside her, kneeling down. Close enough, unfortunately, to see the tears dripping slowly down her face.

"No," she said. "Probably some kid's crush…" And the disappointments, lining on top of each other, were getting harder to take.

Hudson picked up the paper. Was looking at it with the same intent he'd been giving the ground around the orange tree.

Had he been humoring her all along? It was just a cheap copy of someone's profile picture…at worst, some post that had gone viral at school.

Hope had brought more than one of them home from school. Things kids had printed out and passed around, usually as a prank, in lieu of sharing it on their social media accounts and thus leaving a trail for administrators to track and hand out detentions…

"Kids do that," she said to Hudson, figuring he wouldn't be in the know in terms of current social trends among adolescents.

He shook his head. Looked at her.

"I have to call Crosby," he said. "And John."

"Why?" She wouldn't let him look away from her. "What does that picture have to do with Hope?"

The way he was looking at that picture…she would rather him have been humoring her.

"I found a name on her computer," he said. "There was a message, too, but I found it in some coding on a sector, not in an app. I'm not even sure Hope was the one conversing with the girl, or ever saw the message. It was embedded in code."

Yeah, she'd gotten that part.

"The girl's name was Julie, Manda. Julie Poppet."

There were only four letters of the girl's name visible on the little ripped piece of paper. *J-u-l-i.* She felt hot. Nauseous. Started to shiver.

"You think she's with another girl?" she asked him, trying to come up with a scenario that would end happily there. "That they ran away together?"

Or cut school for some other reason that she couldn't fathom at that moment.

She racked her brain trying to think of any Julie Hope had ever mentioned. Came up empty.

Hudson didn't answer her. Just pulled out his phone and dialed.

A few seconds into the conversation, he told someone that there'd been no one named Julie Poppet on any of Hope's friends lists, contacts, church associates or messaging apps, or in her school yearbooks.

From the other parts she heard of his conversations, she figured out pretty quickly that the authorities weren't so much worried about Hope having run away anymore.

They were more concerned that someone had lured more than one girl into a trap—and that those girls hadn't left that park of their own free will.

Amanda's mother's intuition had led her to the park.

She was the one who'd found the photo.

She'd known she had to do something.

She hadn't known she'd be confirming that her daughter's life could be in serious danger.

Oh, God, no. She hadn't known that.

She'd gone to the park to find Hope. Not to lose her.

Hudson ended his call.

Knees weak, starting to feel a little light-headed, Amanda didn't balk when he slid an arm around her waist and headed back toward the parking lot.

She could take care of herself.

But I need help taking care of our daughter.

Chapter 8

Hudson's first instinct, to protect Amanda from as much of the worry as he could, won out for a second or two after he hung up the phone. The one that told him to take her hand, to put an arm around her as they walked back to his car.

"Detective Wedbush is doing a search for Julie Poppet." He told her the easiest first. "While she likely won't be in any of the regular databases, unless she's had dealings with child services, she should show up in birth records. More quickly if she was born in Arizona." And quickest of all if she'd already been the subject of a missing child report, which was why Wedbush was putting out a bulletin to all law enforcement agencies across the state first, requesting information on the girl.

Because Wedbush had only been sharing a possible

theory, not fact, Hudson kept that last piece of the conversation to himself.

He waited until they were in the car, so she'd be sitting down, before he told her the next part. "John got through another sector of the hard drive," he said, his key in the ignition. "He found another message in coding that appears to be a response to the original message I found. It's from someone named Tabitha Blake. Have you ever heard of her?"

Eyes wide, she stared at him. Shook her head. And Hudson dialed Wedbush back to add the girl's name to his search, then started the car. He had to get back to Amanda's house as soon as possible. Get back on those computers. There was more there. His gut was telling him so.

And that *more*, depending on when it was found, could mean life or death for those girls. What it all had to do with the Smythes and their hidden bank account, he had no idea. If it turned out the other girls were also connected to illicitly rich family members, or to others who knew about the Smythes' bank account, there should be ransom demands coming.

Should have already been ransom demands.

Unless, as Wedbush had also suggested, they were in the process of picking up the girls and then, when they had them all, would send out their demands...

Whatever was going on, Hudson would search that girl's computer until he found the connection.

Amanda could not lose her child.

She'd come so far. Had taken charge of her life. Had made her own success, and had created a home with real happiness, too.

She'd done far more than he had. Yeah, he'd won an incredible scholarship. Had made everything out of that opportunity, lived far above any means he'd imagined for himself and spent his days using his talents to help make the world a better place.

But his home was…quiet. Housing only him. There was no family. Not even a bird to gawk at him now and then. He'd had relationships. Plenty of them. Two where he let it get to the point of minor commitment. And they'd both ended disastrously. His fault. Commitment meant expectation. Which created demands on him. Emotional demands. The walls had closed in, and he'd bailed.

He could only give so much.

Family took an ability to give it all.

He could see the giving in Amanda's willingness to do whatever it took—even calling the guy who'd walked out on her—to find her daughter. And before that, the sacrifices, taking on single parenthood, still putting herself through college, building a career, providing a nice, safe home, all of it, for Hope.

And he'd had the audacity to tell her that she needed to learn to take care of herself rather than expecting others to take care of her. He'd told her she needed to learn how to give to others.

But he'd taken from her for four years, finding family within their friendship, building them into a couple, and then, when he'd been forced to choose between his full scholarship and a better life for himself, or staying with her and probably scraping by for the rest of his life—he'd bailed. She'd given him the only thing she'd had: herself.

He'd taken.

The irony in that, considering those last harsh words with which he'd left her, stung. A lot.

"Those things I said to you…that last night…they were wrong, Manda," he said as he drove slowly through residential streets, minding the laws, the fact that there were kids at play, when what he needed to do was break every speed limit and get on with the job waiting for him. "We were young, that's all," he said, knowing the words for the truth that they were. And she'd been a lot younger, streetwise, than he'd been.

Having been in the system since he was a little guy, and still carrying harsh memories from life with his mother and the stepfather who'd made both of their lives miserable, he'd grown up a lot faster than her privileged life had required. That didn't make her less than him, though.

"I was selfish," she said, sounding lost. "That scholarship. You'd earned it, and it was the only way for you to be able to use your talents to the best of your abilities. You were being offered free room and board for four years, Hud. For the first time in your life, you'd been given real opportunity. You'd been rewarded for hard work and being a decent, kind guy…and I didn't celebrate for you. I thought only of what it meant in terms of me, knowing full well that I grew up with opportunity. You deserved your turn."

"You were young," he said again, turning a last corner to approach the gate into her community.

What would life have been for them if he'd had what it took to stick around while she'd matured?

He signaled his right turn into the community,

slowed and saw a glint as something came at him. He saw the chrome, veered sharply into gravel and heard the other vehicle pass. An SUV. Black.

"You okay?" he asked, checking out Amanda first as his heart pounded in his chest.

"What was that?" she asked, turning around to look through the back window. The vehicle had rounded the corner and was gone before Hudson had righted his car.

Her eyes wide, shock on her face, she sat there shaking. Instantly, he wanted revenge on whoever had done that to her.

His phone beeped a text before he could respond. Pulling it out, he saw an unfamiliar number, and the words Leave it alone before another Smythe gets hurt.

Hudson called Wedbush.

And, at the detective's direction, got Amanda safely locked in at home.

Another Smythe. Not Smith. *Another Smythe.* Amanda couldn't get the words out of her brain. Did that imply that Hope was a Smythe? And that she was already hurt? Not just in danger of being so?

They'd been in Hudson's car. The message had most likely been for him.

"Because you talked to my dad today," she blurted. She'd been in the office since they returned to the house and Mabel had left, sitting not far from Hudson, looking at lines and lines of mostly gibberish to her on his laptop, while he worked on Hope's larger desktop screen. She couldn't do his job for him, since she had no idea what the coding stuff meant. But if she could pick out any names, any messages in the midst of it, she could save him some time.

They'd been home fifteen minutes and were waiting for the detectives to come take their statements regarding the near-crash at the gate. She'd seen more than Hudson had. Knew the SUV was midsize, new-looking, black with a lot of chrome. It had had a male driver. Dark hair. Broad-shouldered. Big face. White. Not much more than that, though. She hadn't known, when she'd seen him coming, that he'd been going to veer right at them.

Glancing up, she saw Hudson looking at her. "I introduced you. Gave my father your name." Not her mother, just her dad. Although her mother had guessed who he was. "And you asked him all those technical questions."

"So he gets the word to someone and I get a warning? Wouldn't he be more likely to send a warning to whoever has his granddaughter?"

"Not if he thinks she's in no danger," Amanda said, sitting up straighter in the chair she'd pulled in from Hope's desk. She could have taken the armchair in the reading nook in the corner. She'd wanted to be closer to Hudson.

They could have been killed.

Amanda was scared. So scared. Without Hope...

"What if he knows where she is?" she asked. "What if he knows she's okay?"

"How would he have communicated with someone between this morning and this afternoon to arrange a hit on me?"

"A near-hit," she said, hanging on by telling herself that they'd been in no real danger coming home. It had just been a scare. Right?

"And I have no idea. But I believe it's something he would do, and who else would know you're helping me put the word out?"

It made sense. What else it meant, that her own father really was culpable in what was going on, was something she'd have to contemplate, process, at a later date.

Hudson's phone rang, and she saw the name on the caller ID because he held it up to show her before he answered. Jeanine Crosby.

He spoke for a less than a minute, then turned to her.

"An officer will be here soon to take our statements," he said. "And there will be someone sitting on the house, at least for the next few hours. Crosby and Wedbush are heading to the prison." She knew what was coming next wasn't going to be good before he said any more. The change in his expression, the warmth and sorrow in which he'd wrapped her during the years she'd felt like there was nothing to live for…it was there again.

Freezing inside, she saw his mouth move before she heard the words. "Your mom's been in a scuffle," he said.

Not…they've found Hope and it isn't good.

Or…Hope's been hurt.

My mother.

"She's okay, some superficial bruising…"

My mother? Amanda swallowed and tried not to let tears win the battle she was fighting with them. The woman was a traitor to her. She didn't deserve her tears.

But Amanda loved her anyway. Her gaze blurred.

"They're going to talk to her and to your father," Hudson continued as she wallowed in the concerned gaze she'd missed so much after he'd left. "Could be the altercation had nothing to do with our visit, or her telling us about the bank account. Could be it was a warning."

Her mother was hurt because of what she'd told them? "How would anyone in the prison have known what she told us?"

"Investigators started looking into the account as soon as we left her. If someone is watching it from the outside…"

"But how would someone know to go after her? And then warn you?"

His gaze on her was like warm air on the frost filling her veins. "How do they, or your father, at least, communicate with whoever manages the account for him? That's assuming he has someone doing so. Did those individuals get to Hope? Those are all the things I'm trying to find out," he said. "Everything is pointing to some kind of hidden communication, most likely involving Hope's computer." The words struck her heart, but she didn't flinch. Just nodded, needing him to continue.

"It's also possible that your father has some way inside the prison to communicate with your mother, someone he's paying somehow. It's possible he just paid to send a warning to your mother, just in case. He knew the questions I was asking and knew we were going to see her. He had to send the message, keeping her quiet."

"My dad has never ever lifted a hand to my mother." Her parents had done many things, and she blamed her father for most of it, but he wasn't a violent man.

"This is all just theory, Manda. The truth is, we know

what we know. And right now, it isn't enough. We can't fit the pieces together. So we need to find more pieces."

He was right. And staying with her.

Trying his best to help.

Still…her mother "scuffed up" on top of Hope being gone. How could she make this better for her loved ones?

What could she *do*?

And then it hit her. "Another Smythe gets hurt. So the first one was my mother? Not Hope? But if we don't back off, Hope will be next?"

He shook his head. Not an emphatic no. More like a warning that her fear could possibly be true. "No one knows at this point," he told her.

"But it's pretty clear that my folks are involved in Hope's disappearance," she said, remaining upright in the hard wooden chair. "The routing number you found, Mom admitting about the bank account, and now this. All on the same day she disappears? But there's no way my mom would let anything happen to Hope."

Except…she'd thought Patricia would have taken the same care with her own daughter, Amanda, all those years ago. Surely Patricia had seen trouble coming. And she'd done nothing to protect Amanda from what was to come.

Or even to prepare her to cope.

"Hope's a smart girl. She knows how to keep herself safe," she said, more for herself than anything else.

He glanced toward the computer screen. "She's definitely a smart girl." Hudson sounded impressed. She so badly wanted to tell him that her intelligence was come by naturally. After all, she was his daughter.

But Amanda knew that she couldn't distract him from the job at hand. Hudson wouldn't want the distraction.

Mostly, Hope didn't deserve the distraction. If Amanda told him anything before his job was done, she'd be putting her daughter at greater risk.

"But keep in mind, Manda…the rest of it…the routing number, your mother's admission, all of that is happening right now *because* Hope is missing."

He paused as if to sum up everything that had happened since his arrival. "I'm here to find Hope. In my search I just happened to find the routing number. Which led us to the prison, which led to your mom's confession. And maybe to her being scuffed up. And to our near-miss with an SUV as a warning to us to leave the bank account information alone."

"You think the two are separate, then? All of that and Hope? That what just happened to us, to my mom, has nothing to do with Hope?"

She wasn't ready to accept that. If Hope was somewhere under the auspices of her father, she'd be safe. Right?

But if it was the truth…if her parents and their lies and subsequent problems had nothing to do with Hope's disappearance, then they weren't going to find her if all they were doing was looking at the elder Smythes.

"I don't know what to think," he told her. "It's not my job to come up with the theories. My job is to find whatever facts exist to let the rest of them do their jobs to the best of their abilities."

"You're not looking to prove what my parents are or aren't doing. You're looking to find anything that could lead us to Hope, no matter what information it turns up." Because that was the only way to find Hope. To look for her trail. Period. No matter where it led.

"Exactly."

"Thank you." Her words were soft, but they held her heart within them. And then she seemingly turned her focus back to her computer screen, freeing him to return to his until the police arrived.

Still, with everything falling apart around her, she felt a little better. She'd managed without Hudson since the night he'd walked out on her.

But the second she'd needed him, she'd called him, and he'd come to help her.

That mattered.

Chapter 9

Officers had questioned him and Amanda separately regarding the near-accident at the gate to her community, and then, with assurances that a car would be right outside in the event that either of them needed anything, Hudson went back to work. His conversation with Amanda, her questions, her statements…they'd left one big question in his mind.

How was George Smythe communicating with anyone? He'd had a flash of feeling, a confirmation in his gut, that it was up to him to find that answer. That it was within his realm of responsibility.

That finding that answer is the reason I'm here.

Not given to flights of fancy at all, Hudson still listened to gut feelings. Like Amanda's intuition. He'd had strong ones once before, had ignored them, and a friend had died.

He'd known Sierra had been a bit off, that her question to him about computer activity had been odd, but he'd told himself he had to respect her right to privacy.

If only he and the rest of their group of friends, the partners in Sierra's Web, had talked to each other about her before she'd gone missing...

They likely could have prevented her murder.

He hadn't ignored a single gut feeling in the more than a decade that had passed since then.

He had two leads, two ways in. Julie Poppet. And now Tabitha Blake. Julie's photo at the park put her on the top of his critical list.

Tabitha Blake's response to an innocuous conversation about ponytails put her right up there with Julie.

While the police were working on figuring out who the girls were and finding them, it was up to Hudson to figure out what connection they had to Hope.

He got one hell of lot closer when he discovered a tunnel that led him to the dark web. With a sinking feeling, a dread unlike any he'd known in his career, he found his way into the site, only to be led through a series of complex steps that sent him back out to the internet again—as if he'd been there, innocuously, all alone. But he was on a private message site that allowed people to converse without being seen. A person could be on that site and not know that it was essentially being powered by an entity that lived on the dark web.

He couldn't tie the site itself to anything Hope had done. But he could see that the ponytail conversation between Tabitha and Julie had taken place on that site. How it ended up on Hope's computer, he didn't know.

And what did it mean? He didn't know.

Just as he didn't know how that damned foreign bank routing number had gotten there.

What was the link between the two?

An hour before, he'd explained to Amanda that he had to go at the job from a blank slate, not through theories. He had to find only what was there.

And so he put in a quick call to Wedbush's cell, leaving him a message, and went back to work. Amanda had been in and out. He could hear her in the kitchen. She'd said she was going to heat up something for them for dinner.

He hoped she found a glass of wine in there for herself as well. She was at the end of her rope.

And he couldn't take the time to help ease her pain.

That wasn't his job anymore.

Because he'd given it up. Walked away from it.

From her.

And because worrying about her slowed him down in his hunt for Hope.

So he worked, searching for other mentions of Tabitha or Julie on Hope's computer. Looking for a place she'd have interacted with them—or anyone else.

On his own computer, he had to join a total of seven sites to find his way into the site where he'd finally traced the ponytail conversation.

He put in Hope's username and password and pushed Send. Holding his breath. Maybe he'd get lucky due to the kid's propensity for always using the same credentials.

If she were there, they'd be closer to finding her.

But if she were there, the chances would be much

greater that she'd become a victim of internet child exploitation.

The swirling circle he got as the machine searched was just plain cruel at that point.

As a techie, he knew what was coming. Knew that he was going to find Hope on that site.

But when he turned back to the computer, he saw a message telling him that username or password wasn't found.

Because they weren't there? Or because the system knew he'd signed in on another computer and was programmed to reject entry anytime that happened?

So he got to work. He experimented with various usernames and passwords, creating one for himself. He typed it wrong to see if he got the exact same message as he had when typing from Hope's computer. He did.

Could be for any number of reasons.

He was getting nowhere but frustrated, when Amanda came in with a single plate of broiled salmon, a baked potato and fresh seasoned green beans.

"Where's yours?"

"In the kitchen. I don't want to distract you…"

She wasn't going to eat. Or eat enough. Too much alone time was taking its toll on her. Just things he knew. Thoughts that were presenting themselves to him as rapid-fire facts.

"I need your help," he told her. "Suggestions for other usernames or passwords Hope might have made up instead of her usual one. We can work on it while we eat."

With a nod, she left his plate and headed back to the kitchen.

Good. He'd pulled his stuff out of the fire with that

one. Found a way to shut up her friend Hud, to appease him, while still sticking to the job at hand. Hope had been gone for close to ten hours. Darkness had fallen.

And Amanda had to be going crazy with worry. Her little girl out in the dark all alone. With temperatures dropping down into the forties. Not all that cold by some standards. But to a girl born and raised in Arizona—forties would be uncomfortable at best.

As if cold was the worst thing Hope could be facing…

Amanda was back, her plate holding half the amount of food on his. He noticed, but didn't push the issue. Instead, he made room for her plate beside his on the desk, pulling Hope's smaller and much less comfortable wood chair closer. That hard chair would be the only one she'd want. Because it was Hope's chair.

A lot of time had passed since he'd been with Amanda, but deep down, he still knew her. Deep down didn't change no matter how old one got. It was lost sometimes. Or buried. But it didn't change.

He didn't set out to play any kind of game with her. Or to humor her. He just needed her to swallow the food in her mouth before asking a question that would require an answer. So he looked to her plate. "Eat," he said. Took a bite of his own. And when she'd swallowed, he asked for a password suggestion to pair up with Hope's usual username. He wrote it down before typing it so they could keep track.

And didn't get in.

He took another bite. Looked at her plate. And was gratified when she took a bite, too. As though he had some magic way with her.

As though he *still* had some magic way with her. Had the right to use it.

She suggested. He typed. They ate.

He didn't get in.

And so it went for more than half an hour. Their plates were long empty.

He didn't ask where the answers came from. What part of Hope's life might have significance with the things she said. He just wrote. And typed.

Switched from her usual username to new suggestions, paired with her usual password. And got nothing.

Amanda hadn't asked what he'd wanted to drink with dinner. She'd brought iced tea in for both of them. Hers with lemon, his without. He needed something stronger.

Needed a break to clear his head.

Knew that she wasn't going to be okay to just call it a night with Hope still out there someplace. Crosby called to check in and say that officers would be out front all night.

Nothing else. If they'd found out anything from their meetings with either of the Smythes, she didn't say. He called his trusty associate John, who offered to work overtime, much to Hudson's immense gratitude.

"You need to go home," Amanda said when he'd hung up from that last call. "You're not superhuman, Hud. You've been at this all day. And it's pretty clear we're going to need you to be fresh in the morning."

He could see the panic simmering in her gaze. In the pinched look of her cheeks. Her chin. He couldn't hear it in her voice.

She'd definitely grown up.

For a second there, he wished she hadn't. He missed

the girl who'd laid her innards bare for him. Missed the gift of having her trust him that completely.

He was to blame for its loss.

"I'm not going anywhere." It shocked him to realize he hadn't even thought about going home. "I travel all over the country doing jobs," he said. "Not as often as my partners since a lot of what I do can be done remotely, but when I do have to go, it's most often with little notice. I always have a packed overnight bag in the car."

"You can't stay up all night," she told him. "You need to give your eyes a rest."

"I'm not leaving you here alone."

"I can call Mabel back. She offered to stay when we got home earlier. And there are others I can ask."

"But you aren't going to," he told her. "Are you?"

She shook her head.

"I'll go if you really want me to," he said. "But just to the nearest hotel."

The pleading look in her eyes told him what he needed to know. She couldn't seem to commit verbally, though, and he couldn't stay unless she told him it was okay. They weren't a couple anymore, family, or even close friends. They couldn't act on what they read in each other's minds.

"The threat earlier could have been meant for either of us," he said. "The police protection due to that threat is here. It's probably a good idea if I stay."

"I'd like you to."

He didn't want to pressure her, but he was glad she'd made that call. "Then I will."

"Thank you," she said, her gaze giving him a sad

smile he recognized. He'd seen it so many times in the past when she'd been hurting almost more than she could bear. He'd been able to make her feel a little better.

That look had been what had snagged him from day one, sucking him in to her.

Or maybe he'd been sucking her in. Because having her need him…

How could he possibly feel suddenly as though his life had more value than it had just a day before?

He should get back to the computer. But she'd been right. His eyes needed a rest. As did his brain. He was tired.

Didn't want to get sloppy. Miss something.

But how did you walk away when the answer to finding Hope could be in the very next line, or screen?

"The team listed on your website, the co-owners, how did you all find each other, form a company?" Her question distracted him from his mental fatigue.

"We were friends in college." As soon as he said the words, he wanted to retract them. She was already hurting so badly, couldn't possibly be helped by being reminded of how he'd abandoned her and run off to Harkins University in Arkansas for a free ride. How he'd chosen Harkins over her.

Or maybe it was the last thing he wanted *her* to be thinking.

She didn't say any more, but she didn't appear closed off, either. She sat there in her hard-backed chair, hands in her lap, studying him. The black suit she was wearing spoke of her success as a professional woman, and yet, in that moment, she was his Manda. The woman who'd loved him more than he'd ever been loved in his life. Before, or since.

"The name, Sierra's Web. Who's Sierra?"

"She was a friend of ours." He didn't know how much to say, but wanted to tell her. It didn't feel right, her not knowing about the pivotal event that had shaped his entire life.

He wanted her to know Sierra.

She was watching him, as though waiting.

"Tell me about her."

"She was scary smart. And yet innocent, too, somehow, in that she trusted the world to be a good place. Trusted that right would win. Particularly noteworthy because her mother was dead and her father was an alcoholic who was rarely even in touch with her. She just saw the good in things."

He smiled, remembering. He didn't do that enough… allowing the good times with Sierra to come to life. No, for some reason he only let her death motivate him.

"We all met in a communications class," he said, thinking back. Latching on to the good feeling for a minute or two longer. Wanting to share it with Amanda. "We were grouped together and had to spend the semester talking and writing about all kinds of things. Finding ways to share the things that were buried inside us. The difficult things. It got pretty intense sometimes. But our group…we just kind of…bonded." He'd never put the experience into words before. Not like that. Didn't even think about it much. But he wanted Amanda to understand. He wasn't even sure why. "I told them about you. About leaving…"

It had been the hardest moment in his college career, letting that out.

Her eyes glistened, but didn't break contact with his.

"Anyway…fast forward…the next year Sierra was in this sociology class. She was given this assignment, teamed up with a guy she didn't like, and after that she changed. In subtle ways. We each noticed, but no one knew others were noticing little things. It wasn't like we sat around and talked about each other behind our backs. It wasn't until she didn't meet us the last weekend of break, when we were all worried, that we started talking, and when you put everything together, it was pretty clear that something wasn't right. We tried to reach Sierra. No one could find her. We went to the police with all of our 'evidence,' but they made a call to her father, who said he was sure she was fine and that it was like her to go off alone on her breaks—like he'd know. He hadn't been in touch with her for months…" He broke off, shook his head. Knew that sense of helplessness again…

Swallowed. Glanced at his hands. Kept his focus there. "The next week her body turned up in a dumpster." He didn't expect the surge of emotion that swamped him. He'd spoken of Sierra many times over the years. But Amanda…she hit him in a deeper place. Required more of him.

She brought him more alive than he was without her. He wasn't at all sure that was a good thing.

"What happened to her?" Talking to Amanda put him in the abyss, but her voice pulled him out of it some, too. He looked back over at her, sank into the compassion burning from her gaze. Remembered Sierra through his heart, not his head.

"No one knew. We went to our professor with the concerns we'd taken to the police, and she gave them to a detective she'd worked with once before. Sierra had asked me about encryption, for instance, and the detective searched her computer and found evidence of gambling. Our friend Dorian worked at a clinic and saw her there—the detective spoke with the doctor and found out she'd been raped. No one would have known to speak with her doctor if not for Dorian seeing her there. Sierra never let on to any of us that she'd been assaulted. We'd all seen her after that night. Winchester, another guy in our group, knew she'd wanted to donate a large amount of cash…"

His friends had all had their special interests, their fields of study…

And a friend so used to taking care of herself that she hadn't come to any of them for help. So in tribute to her, now they spent their lives helping others.

"It turned out that the guy she'd been partnered with in sociology, he'd…drugged her and raped her, but she wouldn't make an official report."

"Oh my God, Hud! I'm so sorry…" Mouth open, Amanda stared at him. And he realized that for the first time that day, she wasn't fully engrossed in fighting images of what could be happening to her daughter…

And yet she didn't need to be hearing about violence against women at the moment.

"She'd found out some things about him, that he was involved in an illegal gambling ring, and had been trying to get proof to take to the police, and instead, got herself killed. He played for the Harkins football team, and him and a buddy, a soccer player, were throwing games and making a load of money…" Thinking back…they'd all been so shocked. Sickened. And saddened. Sierra's life and death had changed them all, irrevocably, forever. They were already connected, but it had bonded them so tightly they knew they'd be a team forever."

He looked at her with all of the intensity inside him. "My friends and I led the police to the truth. Sierra had uncovered an illegal college sports gambling ring. The guy from her sociology class had only been a small player, but Sierra's digging got the attention of a big-time bookie and he had her killed."

"I'm so so sorry, Hud. I just can't… I'm so sorry…" The emotion pouring from Amanda, all over him, un-glued him a bit.

"Sierra was probably the one healthy relationship I've ever had." They weren't the words he'd meant to say. And yet, as he heard them, he knew them to be true.

And saw Amanda blanch, but she recovered quickly.

He had a feeling she already knew all the answers where their past was concerned and why it was so un-healthy. He was the one slow on the uptake. Only now he was discovering that his perspective, while valid, had been a snippet. Not the whole picture by a long shot.

And not something he could take on at the moment. He had at least one thirteen-year-old girl to find.

Chapter 10

Sierra was probably the one healthy relationship I've ever had. Amanda's mind played the words back again and again.

Not blaming Hudson for them or even taking offense. When she'd known him, they'd been traumatized kids—her more than him, granted—living in a children's home. They'd been young adults with no real parental supervision, guided mostly by teachers, social workers and a couple of house mothers who oversaw loads of kids. Neither of them had had a healthy example of what a relationship was supposed to look like, though they'd both known things that hadn't worked, by looking at their own parents.

She didn't blame Hudson for anything that had happened, then or later. But the words stung. Because he'd loved after her.

The realization didn't make her proud. Instead of being glad that he'd found love, that he'd had a good relationship, there she was again, making it about her.

Being hurt because he'd moved on.

And she hadn't.

Not from him. She'd never met a man who moved her like he had. But then, having and raising his child had kept her bound to him. At least in her mind and heart where the secret lived free.

And the moment wasn't about her. He wasn't there because of her.

He was there to save their daughter. Even if he didn't know that was who he was saving.

Hope came first.

And so she sat with him, bearing her own pains silently, trying to figure out usernames. Passwords. Talking to him about Hope in an attempt to give him insights into the person whose world he was invading.

Nothing worked. And when he went into the app under the new account he'd made up and searched for either Julie Poppet or Tabitha Blake, he came up blank there, too.

So he went back to looking for hackers, for other messages, for anything that would tell him how those messages from unknown girls had appeared on Hope's computer.

Amanda left him to it for a while. Did dishes. Cried some. Stood with her arms wrapped around her middle and stared into nothingness.

She thought about going to bed, but knew she wouldn't. No way she could put on her nightgown and slip under the covers while Hope was God knew where. Experiencing God knew what.

No way she wanted to sleep with Hudson there, either. They'd never spent the night in a bed together. Rules at the home had been really strict. No visitors to bedrooms. The lovemaking they'd done had happened off campus. In the back seat of the old, used car he'd purchased. And on a blanket spread on a mountain plateau.

She wasn't going to sleep.

But *he* should.

Checking the spare room, she verified that the sheets had been changed since Hope's last slumber party and that the attached bathroom had all essentials. She stopped by her room to change out of work clothes and into a pair of dark gray jeggings and her favorite gray-and-white-checked fleece pullover, adjusting the zip tab above where any cleavage would show. And then, barefoot, she made her way back to the office, expecting to find Hudson as she'd left him, peering between the three screens.

He was on the phone instead. She heard his voice, low-toned and yet urgent, just as she entered the room.

Heard him thank someone, announce that he could be reached at Amanda's house, then say goodbye.

He glanced at her as she came in. Didn't seem to notice that she'd changed. He hadn't changed, himself. But then, he hadn't been out to his car to get the overnight bag he'd said was always packed there.

"Two things," he told her. Standing, he stretched, and she ached for how tired he looked. "First, I've called a couple of my co-owners. You'd said earlier that whatever it took…"

"Right." She nodded. "That's fine. I don't care how much it costs. I'll pay."

His blink, the quick frown, didn't prepare her for his next words. "I'm not charging you, Manda. No way. I'm just letting you know that a couple of my friends are headed this way."

She stared. "Your friends are flying in to help?"

He nodded. "They all know about you." He'd said he'd talked about her in the communications class. She'd wanted badly to know what he'd told them, but she hadn't asked.

"Mariah and Winchester are both just coming off jobs and want to help. Win's our financial wizard. He's already looking into your parents' case. Wedbush sent the file to him. And Mariah's a child life specialist with a doctorate in education as well. She's our child trauma specialist and is already studying Hope's social accounts. They'll both sleep on the plane and be here first thing in the morning."

She didn't know what to say. Just stood there gaping like an idiot. It was either that or burst into tears.

"The others have all been in touch," he added. "They're on other jobs, but will be available to consult…"

Wow. That was family.

Hudson might never have married, but he'd certainly built a family of his own.

She was happy for him. Proud of him.

And overwhelmed, too. "I don't know how to thank you all."

His face straight, serious, he stood there with the

desk between them, and said, "I owe you, Manda. I deserted you cold turkey and took off without another word. I never let you know how to find me, contact me. Never sent a phone number. After four years of telling you I was there for you, I just vanished."

Yeah, he had. But she'd found him. It hadn't been hard. For one, she'd known he was at Harkins. When she'd first found out she was pregnant, she'd thought about contacting him.

She hadn't gotten pregnant on purpose. They'd used birth control. She'd been panicked when she'd first found out she was. But when she'd come to terms with being pregnant, thoughts of getting him back had started to pop into her head. Of making him come back to her. She'd win.

She'd had a strong mental reaction. She'd come face-to-face with the validity of what he'd said to her when he'd left. He'd been right: she thought in terms of herself. Even when she was bringing a new life into the world.

She vowed, then and there, to not be that selfish, privileged little person. And she'd never fallen back.

He was watching her. She held his gaze. Both of them looking around the many things that weren't being said between them.

"You said you had two points." She took another step into the room. Tired, and yet geared up, too.

"I found a hacker on Hope's computer."

"What?!" Hurrying over, as though she could look at the screen and see the face of whoever had her daughter, she stopped just short of him. "Where? Who?"

He shook his head. "I don't know yet," he told her.

"And I don't know that it has anything to do with her disappearance. But someone has been using her email address to send and receive emails. They're routing through her computer, but not showing up in her inbox or sent items folders. The thing is, I don't think she ever saw them, Manda. I don't think she ever knew. This kind of thing happens. Your email is hacked and someone sends something bogus to your contact list, and you don't know. It's a common scam and might not mean anything. I've got John trying to reconstruct messages now, and to trace where they came from or went. And I've let Wedbush know."

"But whoever was doing it…you think that's what put her in danger?"

He shook his head. "Not if it's just a scammer."

"But it could be more."

"Anything could be more."

She nodded. "You need to get some rest."

"I need to find your daughter, Amanda. I owe you."

Oh, he so didn't. And with his IT expert friends looking into things beyond Hope's computer, like her school records, for example…or if their medical expert needed to speak with Hope's doctor for some reason…

Hope's birth date would be brought to Hudson's attention. She'd known that when she'd called him that morning. But when he'd jumped onto the computer, not wanting to know more about Hope…and because he wasn't a detective investigating every part of the case… putting off telling him the truth had been possible.

And it was the right thing to do for Hope's sake, so he wasn't distracted…

But she couldn't let him find out from one of his friends. It was time.

"You don't owe me anything, Hudson," she said slowly. "To the contrary, I owe you."

She walked out of the room. When he followed, she led him to the living room. To Hope's baby book.

How did you tell a man that the child he'd spent the day looking for was his own? How did you tell him you'd robbed him of the first almost fourteen years of her life?

That his daughter had been robbed of knowing him?

How did you tell him if he didn't find her, if the police didn't find her, he might not *ever* get to know her?

How did you tell the man who'd been the love of your life something that you knew would make him hate you?

"What do you mean, you owe *me*?" He stood at the entry to the living room, watching as she took a seat on the couch, baby book in hand.

"Sit down, Hudson," she said, trembling, poised on the brink of having her life change forever. Hope could walk in the door ten minutes from then, healthy, fine, with some kind of great explanation, and life would still never be the same again.

Because once Hudson knew he had a daughter, there was no way he was going to let Amanda have her all to herself.

The Hudson she'd known would probably have walked away. Or opted not to walk back in.

But the man who was slowly approaching her couch, sitting down close enough that she felt the dip in the cushions, would not turn his back on his daughter.

Just like he hadn't turned it on Sierra.

Sierra had been the one to change Hudson's life, just as he'd changed Amanda's.

He's about to change it again.

"What's going on, Manda?"

He was looking at her, not the book in her hands.

Reaching as far as she could within her, searching for a strength she couldn't seem to find, she handed him the book.

And waited.

Hudson took the book. But he didn't open it. He looked at her—her expression beaten. He didn't get it.

"Manda?"

She nodded toward the book. Only because he was following the nod, he glanced down. "My Baby Book," he read on the padded pink cover.

She was showing him her baby book?

As though that would somehow explain why she thought she owed him, not vice versa.

He was exhausted. Mentally, physically, and emotionally, too. Seeing her again, experiencing a resurgence of emotions he'd truly thought only a product of extreme youth and living in a children's home, had made the day rougher.

The current job—finding Hope—was difficult enough.

"Tell me why you think you owe me," he said, meeting her gaze and needing her to help him out.

Her chin trembled, but she didn't speak. Just glanced down again.

"You're not a Smythe by birth?" Or there was some other secret about her life that she'd been keeping from him? Nothing came to mind that would make any difference to him.

Or to their current situation.

He didn't really care who'd borne her, or where she'd come from when she'd landed in the children's home. He'd fallen for the person she'd been there.

And was pretty sure he could fall for the person she'd become since, too, if he'd let himself.

He wouldn't. He couldn't. He sucked at relationships, and he damn straight wasn't going to hurt Amanda again.

"It's not my baby book." She spoke the words almost in slow motion. Or he heard them that way. Aware. And yet still not mentally processing.

Something big was coming. He hadn't caught on in the past few minutes, but he got it then. Glancing from her to the book cover, back and forth a couple of times, he finally opened it.

Read the first page.

It was Hope's baby book. Her middle name was Marie.

Amanda had given her daughter her own adopted spelling of their last name. Smith.

There was a picture of them both. Amanda in the hospital bed, holding a newborn on her chest. Her blond hair spilling all over the pillows upon which she was propped. Her face slightly red, sweaty, devoid of all makeup.

And looking radiant.

He glanced at her. There was no radiance on that face now. She looked pinched to the point of him thinking she was getting sick. Worry etched over every feature.

She owed him?

He turned the page. Read the birth details. Twice. Three times.

The baby's birth weight was seven pounds. Twenty-six inches long. Born at 2:58 in the morning.

On a Saturday.

During his freshman year of college.

Almost exactly eight months after he'd left Arizona.

He didn't move.

Couldn't.

Just sat there.

Dumb.

A stupid man.

A very stupid man.

He couldn't even comprehend how stupid.

On what levels.

He couldn't look up, either. He didn't want to see Amanda's face. Didn't want to read her thoughts or feel her emotions.

He read it again.

The baby who'd been born was thirteen, just as he'd thought all day. But she'd be turning fourteen in less than a month, not in almost a year as he'd thought. Add to that the eight months Amanda had been pregnant after he'd left and it all fit exactly into the time since he'd seen her.

He got the math.

Oh yeah, he got the math.

Boy did he get the math.

"She's mine."

Chapter 11

She's mine. An announcement. Not a question.

Tears streaming down her cheeks, Amanda said, "Yes." Years' worth of pent-up words roiled around inside her. Stories she'd told him only in her mind. Memories she'd stored up in the event he was ever back in their lives, when—to her best estimation—Hope grew up and set about finding him. She didn't need to speak any of it. The book, starting with birth and still ongoing, contained most of it. A journal of things she'd wanted him to know.

He turned a page. And then another. He could see all the firsts.

"This entire day...I've been searching for clues to my own daughter's whereabouts."

Another statement that was bearing, perhaps, a hint of anger.

She deserved more than a hint. She wiped her eyes and prepared to accept whatever was coming to her.

She'd had her reasons. Her justifications. She'd made choices with his best interests in mind. And, she thought, Hope's.

She just hadn't realized, at the time, what she was robbing him of. After all, Amanda hadn't known how all-encompassing and completely fulfilling it was to be a parent. Her own parents had hired people to do everything for her, while they'd lived their lives. She'd had no example of the unbelievable wealth of love and happiness a child brought to a family.

He wasn't turning pages anymore. He was just sitting there, staring at the book. Then he was looking at her, his steely eyes topped by brows furrowed in disbelief. "Hope is mine?"

She wanted to glance away but didn't. Forcing herself to look him straight in the eye, she simply repeated her earlier assurance. "Yes."

"You were pregnant when I left."

"Only about a month. I didn't know." The fact seemed important to her. "I wasn't begging you to stay with me, crying about my lack of a part in your plans, because I was pregnant. I was just being the immature, selfish, privileged girl you said I was."

"I was…" He shook his head. They'd already been over all that. Couldn't change who they'd been.

"And all the years since…" He shook his head. "I can't… It doesn't matter right now. We have to find her." A strange glint covered that dark brown gaze then. It wasn't pointed. More like…awash with tears.

"I know," she said. "And I didn't intend to tell you

until afterward, so you weren't distracted. But with your friends coming…looking into things you wouldn't find on her computer…I didn't want you to hear from them." She'd made the decisions she thought best. Maybe they hadn't always been.

Or maybe there just hadn't been any easy answers.

He still held the book open between his hands. Kept shaking his head. She so badly wanted to comfort him.

But she was the one instilling the hurt instead.

"I find out I have a daughter only to know that she's… out there…that I can't…"

Helplessness weakened her again. She slumped, feeling his despair and sharing it in silence. And yet, completely apart from him, too. Unable to find him. Minutes passed.

She remained still. Just there. Prepared to be there all night.

"I know why you made the choices you did back then." He broke the silence, his tone low and almost defeated-sounding. "But all these years…how long have you known I was back in town?"

She'd promised herself when the day came, she'd be completely honest with him. There'd be no sparing herself. "Six months," she said. She hadn't kept track of her own daughter's father. "When Hope got so bothered that she didn't have family…that class assignment really set her off…I was kind of thrown for a loop. I thought about telling her about you. But she's so impressionable right now, so emotional with her hormones kicking in, and I couldn't take a chance that you'd walk away from her…"

"You took her to see your parents instead."

Yeah, she could see how bad that choice looked at the moment. How bad it had *been*. Choosing them over him. And then calling him to come clean up her mess.

Please, God, let him clean up my mess.

"I've been in touch with them all along," she told him. "They're my family. And until today, I thought they'd come clean. That they'd changed." She wasn't excusing, justifying. Or looking for exoneration. She was explaining. She'd promised herself she'd give him the truth.

The reminder was like a broken record. Repeating itself over and over and over. *The truth. The truth. The truth.*

"And they really don't know I'm her father?"

"No one does." Keeping a secret for more than fourteen years wore on a person. Now it was done. From that point on, there would be only the truth.

While she couldn't help biology, she would not be her parents' daughter in action.

There was relief in having it done.

He glanced at her again. Studying her now. More of a stranger than he'd ever been. It was as though something between them had died that night. Died right there on her couch.

They shared a daughter. But in giving him that news, she'd severed the bond they'd shared. One she hadn't even known still existed until that morning.

She hated the tears that filled her eyes. Hated the weakness.

And hated what she knew they'd do to him.

His own eyes glazed again. Then he turned back to

the book. He closed it, but kept it very clearly in his possession as he slid it under his arm.

"I can't forgive you for this." There was no big outburst. No throwing of blame.

She'd have preferred either to the finality he gave her instead.

"I know."

He stood and she didn't. She sat on that couch, pulling a pillow to her chest, hugging it tight, as she watched him leave the room.

After all, Hudson had always been the walkaway guy. He knew he was giving Amanda a repeat of his performance all those years before, but he did it anyway. Better that than unload on her.

Some recrimination she'd deserve.

But he wasn't sure he'd only dish out what she deserved. Wasn't sure of much of anything. He had to get out. Suck fresh air into his lungs.

Have only the sky above him.

Or maybe he should get in his car and drive. Just go. Didn't matter where. What road he took. Just had to go.

His gaze passed across Amanda's laptop, and he burned, thinking of her using it to look him up.

Finding him. Right there.

And not letting him know…not letting Hope know…

How dare she?

He'd actually had biological family of his own, and she hadn't let him know?

Hope. He'd missed so much. Lost chances that would never come again. Choking up, he blinked.

Hope's computer loomed, and he stared at it, her

book still clutched tightly beneath his arm. The book Amanda had kept up to date, chronicling every aspect of their daughter's life.

For him?

Didn't matter.

She'd found him and hadn't called. Hadn't told Hope she had a father. And now Hope was in danger, and he didn't know what she needed.

Amanda had had no right to keep his child, his own family, from him…

Hope. A tear dripped out. He brushed it off, swallowed the lump in his throat.

That sweet, innocent, smart and tech-savvy young woman was his daughter. His flesh and blood.

He was a father…and his daughter was missing.

Emotion swarmed him, buzzing and attacking. Regret. Anger. Fear. And a love so deep, so burning, he couldn't let it out.

He had to get out.

Leaving the computers, he strode back through the living room and out the front door. Only then he considered the cop car there, the officers inside it, watching the house.

Because they were all in the middle of a crisis much more pertinent than the personal one he'd just been thrown into. Waving, he pointed to his car. A uniformed, short-haired, medium-height man exited the cop car, approaching him with weapon in hand.

"I'm just getting my bag," Hudson said. "I'm sorry. I should have called." They'd been given the cell numbers of both officers.

"It's okay, sir. You're sure everything is all right in there?"

"Yes." By their standards it was. There was no danger lurking in Amanda's house. Only heartbreak. He pulled out his big overnight duffel, unzipped it enough to show the man pajamas and clean clothes. Not that he'd asked.

But Hudson wasn't leaving anything to chance.

Not anymore. He had a thirteen-year-old daughter.

He was a father. And his girl needed saving.

He had a job to do. And he was good at it. One of the best.

Until the job was done, he would be focused. On.

And afterward…he had no idea. None. Couldn't even contemplate an afterward.

Except to know that he couldn't just walk away from this one.

Amanda heard Hudson get his keys and cried when she heard the front door close behind him. Not quiet tears, but hard, wracking sobs. Everything she'd been pushing back throughout that long agonizing day and evening came bursting forth at once in howls. Animalistic eruptions of the pain that was consuming her. She let it come. Didn't even try to hold on. To fight.

At that moment, all she could do was feel.

Hurt.

Grieve.

Until she heard the front door open. Heard footsteps, the rustling of something being brought in hitting the doorjamb. And she pushed back the anguish.

It was hers alone.

Brought on, probably in large part, by her.

To be dealt with alone.

But there was more to life. There was Hope.

And she had to have hope.

Even in her deepest grief, she'd held on to that.

To hope.

She'd raised a smart, strong young woman. A survivor. Hope would meet her father one day. Amanda had to believe that.

What their lives might look like after that, with Hudson in Hope's life, she didn't know. And wouldn't try to control.

What it would look like would be whatever the two of them designed it to look like. She'd support them through it. No matter what it was.

He didn't stop in the living room. Went straight back to the bedroom she'd mentioned to him for his use earlier in the evening. Way earlier. Had it only been hours since Hope's disappearance? Since Hudson's re-entrance in her life? In some ways it seemed like days. A week or more.

A minute or two later he was in the hall again. Heading out to her?

Picturing the shock and utter devastation on his face as he'd looked at her after realizing that Hope was his... tears filled her eyes again. Not for her, but for him.

She'd hurt him so deeply.

And had never wanted to do so.

She'd loved the man with her entire being.

And suspected that she probably still did.

Turning off the light beside her, the only one on

in the room, she sat there in the dark, knowing she wouldn't sleep.

"Have there been other men in her life?" The question came from the archway between the living room and the hall. Not far from the door to the office. "Father figures?"

"No." And then, looking for total truth, "Maybe. Her friends' fathers. A tennis coach when she was ten. His son was one of her friends from tennis camp. They moved away later that year."

"And here at home…you're an attractive woman… I'm sure you've dated…"

He didn't come into the room. Just stood in the hall-way. Her accuser.

She was on trial in her own home. And understood, too. He had a right to the answers he sought. His manner—considering the untenable circumstances—was almost admirable.

"Actually, no, Hudson, I haven't really dated. I've been out to dinner on occasion, have attended brokerage parties and some fundraisers, sometimes with a male companion, but never the same man twice. And not one of them ever came to the house." She'd vowed to tell the truth. And the truth was… "I was open to dating. I'm only thirty-two, and I don't want to live my life alone. I just haven't found anyone who lights that spark."

Not since you.

No other man even came close to igniting within her the depth of emotion Hudson had elicited since day one. Not just passion. Or attraction. In the early days, there'd been some of that, of course. She'd been fourteen. Hormonal. But they hadn't even had sex until they were eighteen. Their bond…it had gone way deeper than that.

For her, at least.

He'd moved on to Sierra not long after he'd left her.

Jealousy sprang forth, putting hurtful words on the tip of her tongue, but she didn't let them get the better of her. Didn't let them out. Lashing out at him wouldn't do anyone any good.

Least of all Hope.

And the way he'd felt…for her, or for Sierra…you couldn't help that. The love was there, or it wasn't. Trying to make it there, when it wasn't, was a recipe for disaster, too.

He hadn't responded.

When she turned, looking through the shadows to the hall, he was gone.

Chapter 12

At some point that night, Amanda dozed off. She awoke once to see a shadow in the armchair not far from the couch. Recognized Hudson, in sweats and a T-shirt, with his head back and mouth hanging open.

She'd forgotten that he slept with his mouth open. But had a flash memory of teasing him about it after he'd fallen asleep on a couch during a ballgame several of the kids had been watching one Sunday afternoon.

With a tired smile on her face, she fell back to sleep. Secure in the knowledge that both of Hope's parents were going to do all they could for her.

And that one way or another, they'd be there for her when she came back to them.

When she awoke again, just after five, it was still dark outside. And there was no sign of Hudson. Not in the chair. Not even of him having been there.

FREE BOOKS GIVEAWAY

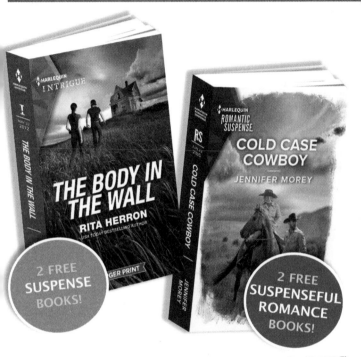

GET UP TO FOUR FREE BOOKS & TWO FREE GIFTS WORTH OVER $20!

We pay for everything!

See Details Inside

YOU pick your books –
WE pay for everything.
You get up to FOUR New Books and TWO Mystery Gifts...absolutely FREE

Dear Reader,

I am writing to announce the launch of a huge **FREE BOOKS GIVEAWAY**... and to let you know that YOU are entitled to choose up to FOUR fantastic books that WE pay for.

Try **Harlequin® Romantic Suspense** books featuring heart-racing page-turners with unexpected plot twists and irresistible chemistry that will keep you guessing to the very end.

Try **Harlequin Intrigue® Larger-Print** books featuring action-packed stories that will keep you on the edge of your seat. Solve the crime and deliver justice at all costs.

Or TRY BOTH!

In return, we ask just one favor: Would you please participate in our brief Reader Survey? We'd love to hear from you.

This FREE BOOKS GIVEAWAY means that your introductory shipment is completely free, even the shipping! If you decide to continue, you can look forward to curated monthly shipments of brand-new books from your selected series, always at a discount off the cover price! Plus you can cancel any time. Who could pass up a deal like that?

Sincerely

Pam Powers

Pam Powers
For Harlequin Reader Service

Complete the survey below and return it today to receive up to **4 FREE BOOKS** and **FREE GIFTS** guaranteed!

FREE BOOKS GIVEAWAY
Reader Survey

1

Do you prefer stories with suspenseful storylines?

◯ YES ◯ NO

2

Do you share your favorite books with friends?

◯ YES ◯ NO

3

Do you often choose to read instead of watching TV?

◯ YES ◯ NO

YES! Please send me my Free Rewards, consisting of **2 Free Books from each series I select** and **Free Mystery Gifts**. I understand that I am under no obligation to buy anything, no purchase necessary see terms and conditions for details.

❏ Harlequin® Romantic Suspense (240/340 HDL GRRU)
❏ Harlequin Intrigue® Larger-Print (199/399 HDL GRRU)
❏ Try Both (240/340 & 199/399 HDL GRR6)

FIRST NAME   LAST NAME

ADDRESS

APT.#   CITY

STATE/PROV.   ZIP/POSTAL CODE

EMAIL ❏ Please check this box if you would like to receive newsletters and promotional emails from Harlequin Enterprises ULC and its affiliates. You can unsubscribe anytime.

HI/HRS-122-FBG22

BUSINESS REPLY MAIL
FIRST-CLASS MAIL   PERMIT NO. 717   BUFFALO, NY

POSTAGE WILL BE PAID BY ADDRESSEE

HARLEQUIN READER SERVICE
PO BOX 1341
BUFFALO NY 14240-8571

NO POSTAGE
NECESSARY
IF MAILED
IN THE
UNITED STATES

For a second, she wondered if she'd dreamed him there, but remembering that open mouth, she knew she hadn't, and went in to take a shower.

She did fine with the routine, right up until she had to choose what to wear. Standing in her walk-in closet, wrapped in her towel, she stared at the clothes hanging there, started to panic and then to cry. She didn't know what to wear. Didn't know what the day was going to bring.

Fear controlled her for the couple of seconds it took her to see what was happening, and then she straightened. Grabbed her favorite long tunic sweater—favorite because while it looked professional enough to wear to work, it was as soft as pajamas. The formfitting black-and-white-striped top hung halfway down her thighs, belted at the waist and went perfectly with her favorite pair of black leggings. Slipping into black flats, she didn't even bother with her last cursory check in the mirror before leaving her room.

She was not at all ready for the day. She'd be meeting Hudson's friends. People who'd known him for a longer period of time, and knew him better, than she did. People who'd known Sierra. Known him when he'd been with Sierra.

And that was the least of what that day was going to hold. She was standing tall, but mostly held up by the tension laced through her. Hope had to be there before another night passed.

If she wasn't…

Statistics said the first twenty-four hours…

And there were only three and a half of those left.

She never should have gone to sleep. She'd lost a few precious hours...

Of praying and willing her daughter home.

Hudson, who'd presumably also showered, and was wearing black pants with an off-white, slightly wrinkled button-down shirt with the tail hanging out, was already in the office, at the desk, typing, when she found him.

He'd made coffee. She had a cup in her hand. But most pressingly, she needed to tell him how sorry she was.

She would have liked to be able to tell him she'd made a huge mistake. That if she'd had it to do over again, she'd have tried to find him, called him, as soon as she found out she was pregnant. But she couldn't do that.

The truth was, if she had it to do over again, she'd make the same choice as she'd made back then. She'd probably make *all* of the same choices.

Because she'd done what she'd thought best at the time.

He glanced up as she came in. Went back to typing. And then, apparently finishing what he'd been doing, sat back.

"I spoke to Wedbush while you were in the shower."

He'd have heard the shower. Or he could have come looking for her...

They'd never shared a space with a shower before. There'd been boys' dorms and girls' dorms. And those secured hallways were never visited by the opposite sex. Not ever.

What she'd give to have Hope behind doors as secure as those had been. She wasn't ready to hear what Wedbush had to say.

Wasn't ready to face the day.

"And?"

His gaze landed on her, met with hers fully. And it wasn't completely empty. She held on to the little bit of him she could see there. Held on tight as he said, "There is no record of a Julie Poppet anywhere. Not in missing persons, not in birth records. People stayed up all night searching national databases and no child aged nine to sixteen was born with that name."

She'd never heard the last name of Poppet. "So what does that mean?"

"That we're dealing with someone using an assumed name."

"And Tabitha?"

"There was a Tabitha Blake. She lives in North Dakota, is twenty-three and is rarely on the internet. Officers were sent to speak with her. She'd never heard of Julie Poppet, nor had she ever had a conversation online regarding ponytails. She also hadn't ever heard of the site where we think the supposed girls were meeting."

She understood that hint of warmth in his gaze. He might not consider her a friend anymore, but he was human. And had known the news was going to be hard for her.

"So, we're nowhere," she said. And realized, as she said *we*, that the word had a whole new meaning. She was no longer the only parent worried sick about Hope. They were together in that.

"We're right where we were," he said, finally breaking eye contact with her. "Just no further ahead."

And with the time passing, that meant they were further behind.

"Wedbush also advised that we not go anywhere for the time being. They're sending a new team of officers to keep a watch on the place. My friends caught flights with similar arrival times and will be renting a car. They're going to stop here—I gave them the neighborhood gate code. After we meet, they'll head to the police station. Wedbush and Crosby will take it from there, getting them up to speed."

The almost robotic tone hid what he wasn't letting her see.

"I'm so, so sorry, Hud," she said, forcing back the tears. She knew her own pain intimately, but could only imagine the scope of his. Finding out he had a daughter in the middle of an investigation for a missing child. Finding out about her and not being able to find her. "You should never have to be meeting her this way..." Through a baby book. Her computer. Investigative information.

"Let's just pray I get to meet her," he said, his voice gruff, as he turned his attention back to his computer. He wasn't going to let her in. Let her help him.

With a new wave of fear striking her heart, Amanda went to make breakfast.

Hudson met his friends out front, intending to fill them in from his perspective and let them get on their way to the police station. Hope needed them far more than he did at the moment.

Still, hugging them both as they got out of the rental

car, he was thankful they'd come. There was no time to waste.

And something they had to know.

Looking at them both, Win with his short-cropped black hair and shirt and tie, and Mariah, with her long red curls and fair skin, he tried to be businesslike and instead just blurted, "She's my daughter." The words, so unfamiliar, so much not a part of any realm of his life, flew out of him. "She's my daughter, guys. We have to find her before it's too late. I haven't even met her yet." It just poured out. The things he'd been trying not to think about. Things he couldn't process.

"She's your…" Win started in, as Mariah said, "She's your what?!" cutting him off.

Both were frowning, clearly stunned.

"Amanda was pregnant when I left for college," he said. "I didn't know."

"When did you find out?" Mariah's concern was evident, and he was thankful all over again. His friends had been there for him for over a dozen years.

"Last night." He told them about the book. About reading the whole thing the night before. As Mariah and Win soaked up his words, patting him on the shoulder, giving him another hug, he realized something else. He had them. And the others. They'd built lives, careers, a successful business, all together.

And Amanda had made a success of herself, while raising a daughter, all alone.

That didn't make her keeping Hope from him right. Whatever his choices might have been, he'd had as much right to make one as she had.

But he'd never bothered to contact her or to tell her

how to contact him. He'd walked away on purpose, meaning to have nothing more to do with her.

He'd had a right to know he had a daughter. But now, he needed his full focus on finding Hope—not on dealing with who she was.

He and Amanda had to be on the same side on this one, working together.

How did you go about your day when your child was missing? Amanda struggled to find purpose. Other than providing a hot breakfast for her and Hudson, eaten in separate rooms, she was at a loss. She kept replaying conversations she'd had with Hope, trying to remember anything and everything that was said during visits with her parents.

She was attempting not to think of her parents other than in terms of any influence they'd had on her daughter.

So much she wanted to force herself not to think about. Had to fight with her brain constantly to keep it on track—a feat made more difficult by the fact that she had no clear track on which to keep it. She just had to keep scanning for anything she could think of that might be a clue to Hope's whereabouts.

And to keep her mind off Hud. He was there. Giving his all to finding their daughter. And she was eternally grateful for that.

She'd lost his friendship, obviously, but in reality that had been gone long before Hope had disappeared. She was the only one who'd clung to what they'd been. Truth was, she was probably the only one who'd been so deeply connected. The only one who'd found the love of her life.

She'd hoped to meet his friends when they'd stopped by, but he'd clearly avoided that—heading outside to meet them. She'd had one quick peek out the window, to see Hud hugging two strangers in her driveway, and something inside her had shut down at the sight.

They'd seen each other for the first time in so many years and she'd barely gotten a handshake, let alone a hug.

He'd moved on.

But Hudson was there. And he had called in his team to help.

She couldn't ask for any more. And would be forever grateful to him. Forever indebted.

He'd given her Hope.

On her early-morning call with Jeanine Crosby, she'd suggested that she wanted to be out, scouring the neighborhoods, driving around looking for any sign of Hope, and had been told, quite sternly, to stay put. They needed to figure out who'd tried to run her and Hudson off the road the evening before. Police resources were already being used to watch over her house. She didn't want to pull any more away from finding Hope.

They were following up on the many tips coming in through the Amber Alert. So far, none of them had panned out, but all it took was one.

A white-collar crime unit had taken over the investigation of her parents' hidden bank account. And there'd been nothing new to connect that account to Hope's disappearance, but they were still following that lead.

Jeanine, as she'd now told Amanda to call her, hadn't

said anything about Julie Poppet being a fake name. She didn't share any theories about why a photo of a fake girl had shown up at her daughter's last known whereabouts and also on her daughter's computer. Or why Julie's conversation with the also-supposedly-fake Tabitha Blake had been on Hope's hard drive.

And Amanda hadn't asked. Theories were just that, theories. Not reality. And she couldn't sit there thinking about her daughter hidden somewhere, being abused at the hands of a predator. To do so would unhinge her, and Hope needed her strong. Hope needed her to not think that way.

And there was no proof that the "Juli" in the photo she'd found was the Julie Poppet on Hope's computer.

No proof that the ponytail conversation with Tabitha had anything to do with Hope's disappearance.

She was in the kitchen, putting the last batch of chocolate pixies in the oven—Hope's favorite cookie—when Hudson appeared just before nine.

The twenty-four-hour mark.

The party casserole that was also Hope's favorite was already prepared and in the refrigerator, ready to be baked.

Coffee cup in hand, Hudson had loaded the single-serve machine and was waiting for the dripping to stop. When it did, though, he didn't leave.

He didn't mention the baked cookies sitting in foil on the counter, filling the kitchen with chocolate aroma. The plan had been twofold. She wanted to remind herself of happier times, memories with Hope. And to have the cookies ready for her daughter's return.

Preparing Hope's loving *welcome home*.

"I found something, Manda."

Manda. The tight clutches on her heart eased some. And at the same time, fear soared.

He'd found something and was standing around making coffee? The thought was instantly followed by... he was the bearer of the news to her. The others, those working the case, already knew.

Putting the dirty, but empty, dough bowl down, she turned to him. "What?"

"I believe your father has been using Hope's email address to communicate with a man named Mack Walters. Do you know him?"

Mack Walters. Uncle Mack? She'd tried to call him once, that first night in the home. He hadn't picked up. The next day she'd been told not to try to contact him again.

"He was my dad's closest friend," she said. "They'd been fraternity brothers. He was one of the first to distance himself from my parents after the Ponzi scheme was discovered."

She didn't get it. "My dad is using Hope's email address?"

"Someone from the prison hacked into her computer and her email account. They sent and received emails that she never knew about. He had them rerouted. Crosby made some calls, and your dad's computer time logins coincide with what I found. I knew your dad was a brilliant financier. I didn't realize he was also a technology expert." He'd certainly feigned ignorance the day before.

Still thinking about the bombshell Hudson had just dropped, Amanda blurted, "Hope's email address? How did he get..." With a start, she remembered. "The first time I took her to see him, he told her he sometimes got email privileges and asked if it would be okay with her if he emailed her. With my permission, she gave him the address. I asked her later if she ever heard from him, and she hadn't."

With my permission. Oh, God, what had she done? What had her father done? And why?

And what did any of it have to do with Hope's disappearance? Or the threat to them the previous evening?

"You'll want to tell Crosby that," Hudson said, still standing there with her as though he planned to stay a minute. "And what you know about Mack Walters, too. She's going to be calling you here shortly."

"My dad's back in touch with Mack?" She just wasn't getting it. Or how Hope had become involved.

"He's been emailing someone using Walters's IP address. Wedbush is bringing Walters in for questioning now. And Crosby is on her way to the prison to see your parents again."

"I thought another team was working on my parents' stuff."

"The bank account part of it. The emails came from Hope's computer, which makes this part of Hope's case."

"Because they still think those emails had something to do with Hope's disappearance." It had been the theory. That her parents were responsible for Hope being gone. "That's why the coding showed up with the routing number, isn't it? It was embedded as part of an email." She knew enough to know that hard drive sectors didn't act like normal filing drawers. Things could be mixed up anywhere.

And she knew that if Hud had traced emails using her daughter's address sent from the prison, her father was involved.

While it made her hate the people who'd given birth to her, the theory that her daughter's disappearance stemmed from them also left hope that her little girl was being held safely someplace.

"I don't get it," she said. "What good does it do them to hold Hope? I haven't received any kind of ransom demand."

"No, but your father might have."

Right. Even in prison, the man had more power than she did. And had the ability to rip her life apart, too.

It was possible her parents weren't behind Hope's disappearance. That it was someone who wanted what they had.

And after her dad gave whoever it was what they wanted, would they attempt to kill Hope? "We've got to find out who's behind this before he gives them what they want," she said aloud, shaking. "I need to see them," she added, her mind skittering all over the place. "I can get them to tell me."

She'd do whatever it took. She didn't know what. But something. She had to do something!

"What did the emails to Mack say?"

"I don't have much," he told her. "John's back up after a few hours' rest and is looking now. I just traced back communication between Hope's email, the prison and an IP address registered to Mack Walters. It was all encrypted—and I suspect that the program was written to erase email content upon encryption being broken." She appreciated him talking in straightforward enough terms that she got the gist of what he was saying, even though she wasn't a techie.

Hudson had always been thoughtful that way. Aware of others' feelings and capabilities. Or lack thereof.

At least, with her he had been.

Once upon a time...

She brought the thoughts to a skidding halt.

"So we'll never know what was being said." She had to stay focused. Stay on track. No matter how much it hurt to look at what a mess life had become.

To see how truly awful her parents really were.

To look at herself visiting them every month all the years since their arrest and wondering how that person hadn't seen...hadn't quit going...

"It's possible that we'll never know." Hudson met her gaze as he gave her what sounded like the unvarnished truth.

It was the first time his eyes had met hers, and held on, since she'd handed him Hope's baby book.

"What we need to focus on, another likely possibility, is that the conversations with your parents, and with Mack Walters, will lead us closer to Hope."

In time. They had to get to her in time.

He didn't say the words.

She heard them anyway.

And for a moment, as they stood there, sharing a mutually unspoken fear, her soul mate Hud was back.

Chapter 13

Amanda rushed into the office where Hud was working half an hour later.

"Look!" She held out her phone open to her text app. "I don't know the number," she said. But the message was clear.

Call the dogs off or your daughter gets hurt.

"It means she hasn't been hurt yet, right?"

Hudson wanted to tell her that was exactly what the text meant. He couldn't lie to her any more than he could lie to himself.

"Your parents know Hope is missing, Manda. Anyone who's threatened by the bank account investigation could have sent that." But he called Wedbush immediately with the number from which the text had come.

And did a quick search himself, from the access he had to certain databases. He wasn't surprised to see, in less than a minute, that the number came from a burner phone.

"We're past the twenty-four-hour mark!" Amanda said, oblivious to his finding. "If she's still alive, that means she's beat statistics…"

He'd been watching the clock as well. Fully understood the panic driving her. It was getting to him, too, which was why he'd called in a third IT person to help with the case. No way he was stepping back, but he was going to have his own back—have someone watching for anything he might miss.

His daughter's life was at stake.

"All we can do is keep being here, Manda. Keep doing what we're doing," he said. "Keep believing that she's going to make it home. Belief is a powerful thing."

He'd seen it in action. Wasn't really sure he bought into its power over the more likely explanation of coincidence when things seemed to come together in an inexplicable way, but he couldn't completely discount it, either. He couldn't prove that believing in something had no power.

She reached for her phone. Sat in the chair she'd occupied the night before. Not right up next to him, but not far away, either.

"It's been twenty-four hours." Her tone was completely different now. Soft. Fear-filled.

He nodded. Hating the helplessness that had been plaguing him since the night before. Weakening him. His first job as a father and he wasn't working miracles. "I know," he told her.

"I can't live without her, Hud."

"Belief, Amanda. It's what you've got to give her right now. You intend to live your life with her in it, put that intention out there." The words were way more like Mariah's, or Sierra's, than his, but out they slid.

Her features relaxed enough that he noticed. She still looked pinched. And alarmingly beautiful. The things the woman did to him...on so many levels...

Didn't bear thinking about.

And yet, in a way, they were keeping him on the right track, too. Driving him to focus on the screen, not on the things he couldn't change.

"I'm afraid, Hud. For her. And for us, too. Whoever is out there, they know we're here. I feel like a fish in a bowl with thin glass."

"That's why we have police protection right outside. And we're in a gated community, too, though I know it's not that difficult to surpass that part. Still, it's something." He looked for everything he could find to comfort her.

The way it had always been with them.

He felt the physical spike of shock as her phone rang. Saw the stark terror in her eyes before she glanced down and saw who was calling. Detective Crosby.

He looked her deeply in the eye, kept her with him and nodded toward the phone.

She answered, putting the call on speaker.

"I need you two to say put, and away from windows," Crosby said. "The officers out front are in pursuit of someone who'd been lurking in the wash behind your house. We've got other teams on the way. Just stay out of sight."

"Okay," Amanda said. "We're in the office. The only window faces the house next door, and it's in clear view of the street, blocked from the back by a six-foot wall." Hudson was amazed at her calm, her clear thinking.

And it dawned on him...her fear, the pain, the anxiety and anguish...none of it was for herself. It was all for Hope. When her own life was in danger, she was a rock. She was a true mother in every sense of the word.

"Get over here," he said, wanting her behind the desk with him. *He* wasn't so much a rock when *Amanda's* life was in danger.

She scooted closer, and he pulled her up and then down to the floor with him, pushing her under the desk while he guarded the front of it.

"I'm already at the prison," Crosby was saying, "but I'll stay on the line until I get notice that you've got protection."

He appreciated that. But... "Do you have any kind of weapon?" he asked Amanda.

When she shook her head, he grabbed a razor blade knife out of his bag. It wasn't much—he used it to help him remove sensitive computer chips—but it would at least slow down anyone who got in the house and tried to hurt Amanda.

"Why would they want me?" she asked.

"Same reason they'd want Hope," Jeanine Crosby said. "To send a message to your parents. If we're lucky, my officers are going to catch the guy, and we'll be that much closer to getting Hope back to you."

Keeping glued to the wall, Hudson listened to Amanda telling Jeanine what she knew about Mack Walters as he moved to the window. Glanced out to see the small area Amanda had described, completely closed in by a wall that stretched from the side of her house, across to the neighbors', with another perpendicular wall separating the two yards, and part of the shared wall enclosing the backyards as well. If a perp got in there, he'd be the sitting duck.

And if he didn't…Amanda would be safe.

The bastards already had his daughter. They weren't getting her mother, too.

"The good news is that they still don't have what they want, so Hope is alive for now, right?" Amanda asked twenty minutes later. The new officers on duty outside had been in the house, looked it over and reported that the guy who'd been lurking had gotten away. Just disappeared. Whether that meant he lived in the neighborhood, or had a way to get in and out undetected, they didn't know. Someone was looking into that as well, and the officers who'd seen him were at the station giving a description, working with a sketch artist in case anything popped on the guy.

"That's what we need to hope," Hudson said. Back at his computer, he had said there was something there that he hadn't found. Yet.

Amanda wanted to ask the longest he'd taken on one job and still managed to bring it to a successful conclusion. He'd already spent so much time on Hope's computer. Was there still something to find?

But she held her tongue.

His friend Winchester had called shortly after they were off the phone with Crosby. His news: there were several million dollars sitting in her parents' hidden bank account. And there'd been regular withdrawals from it, too. Every month since her parents went to prison.

"Someone on a payroll," she'd heard Hudson say. And then, "I'll try to trace it."

Mariah had gone with Crosby to the prison, to talk to her mother about Hope. She was on her way, with Crosby, to see Amanda.

All around her activity was happening. Action was taking place.

And Amanda had to take action, too. She had to consciously work on believing. To work on her intention to have Hope home again.

"Got it," Hudson said. Before he gave her any indication as to what "it" was, he'd speed-dialed Wedbush. Amanda, hurrying over to look at his computer over his shoulder, still had no idea what he'd found.

"The money is going to Walters," he said. "Has been since the Smythe convictions."

She slumped down to the desk. Couldn't believe it. Mack Walters had been so quick to condemn her parents. Publicly. Painfully. To turn on her.

And he has Hope?

"He was stealing from them?" she asked as soon as Hudson hung up. "And my father somehow found out? That would explain the emails. He'd have needed to send them in a way they wouldn't be intercepted. Could have worded it in such a way that if someone saw it outgoing, it wouldn't raise any flags…"

She'd made it all easy for him, delivering his granddaughter up, allowing him to email her. She'd just been trying to give Hope a family.

But the truth was, Hope's family was only a few miles away. A father she'd never met who was working diligently to find her.

"That's why he'd want Hope." It was all making horrifying sense. "My father somehow found out Mack was stealing from him all these years. So Mack took Hope to keep my father quiet. And since we're still looking into things, he's after me, too," she finished, still standing just behind Hudson. He turned, and she found herself almost between his knees. She stepped back and started to stumble. He put his hands on both of her hips, steadying her.

She didn't want to move after that. The contact…it gave her strength. Relief. Was like coming home in the middle of a hellacious storm.

Hudson moved, whether by accident or design, she didn't know, but she lost her footing and ended up sitting on his lap, his arms catching her at first. And then wrapping more completely around her.

Holding her. Tight.

She held him, too. Her arms around him, she pressed her face into his neck, feeling the warmth of his skin. She was giving everything that was broken about her to him. To find acceptance—acceptance in the first place she'd ever truly found it. Felt it.

In his arms.

Lifting her head, she had to see him, to have those chocolate-brown eyes meeting hers openly, taking her in, and giving himself, too. His gaze was there, boring into her with an intensity she didn't recognize, and still, she stayed.

Wanted to be there.

His lips moved, hers did, and they were kissing, tongue to tongue, urgent, rough kisses. Losing air. Gasping. And breathing into each other, too.

Nothing like it had ever been between them before.

She felt him grow beneath her butt. Knew an answering animalistic need within herself.

And...they both pulled back.

Simultaneously, which shouldn't have surprised her, but did.

"That didn't just happen," he said, reaching up to steady her as she quickly stood, but she stepped away from his hands. From him.

She offered a more realistic approach. "Or it did happen because it needed to, and now it's done."

"Good," he said. "Right, that's better," he added, and went back to work.

But not for long. His phone rang almost immediately. As did hers. As she was on the way out of the room. Their gazes met, and he said hello.

Continuing out to the living room, Amanda picked up as well.

Hudson found her out there less than five minutes later. Sitting on the couch. It wasn't even noon yet, and it felt as though they'd lived a week since the night before when she sat in that very same spot and told him that Hope was his daughter.

She was just sitting there, hands clasped on the knees of her black leggings. Staring into space. He knew she'd been talking to Detective Crosby. The call had been from Wedbush, who'd told him so.

He knew what she'd been told.

He also knew he had to be close to her. The past wasn't okay. Things between them weren't okay. But they didn't matter at the moment, either.

"What matters, right now, is the two of us getting through this. Finding our daughter," he said, his throat tightening over the words. More than twelve hours had passed since he'd found out he was searching for his own child, and still the idea was too surreal to fully grasp.

She didn't move. Didn't speak. Didn't look at him. It was as though she was locked inside a self he didn't know. He had no idea how to find her in there.

"Together, Manda. The only way you and I are going to get through this is together. You're…a strength to me right now." Something he'd never seen before. At all. Though he'd begun to realize he'd relied on her back then far more than he'd known. "And I used to be a strength to you…"

She turned her head, her blue eyes moist as they studied him. The rest of her stoic expression didn't change.

"I need you," he said. "Right now," he had to clarify. The only way she was going to believe him, trust him, was if he was as honest as he could be. "And I think maybe you need me. Just until we find her…"

Her lips trembled, and he slid his palm beneath hers, threading their fingers together. "Whatever it takes to get us through this," he said softly.

Leaning forward, she placed her lips against his. A closed-lips, completely sedate gesture. And before she pulled away, he tasted her tears.

"My parents were going before the parole board next year," Amanda said, a stonelike coldness inside her as she sat with Hudson on the couch. Jeanine and Mariah would be there soon. They were picking up lunch for all of them.

Curious to meet Mariah, the woman who'd been a friend to Hudson for more years than Amanda had spent with him, she was mostly just on automatic pilot. Her mind working, her heart on standby.

"They've been communicating through their lawyer all these years. And through a delivery person who services both the male and female facilities," she continued, delivering to Hudson the information she'd just received from the detective. Her mother had given up the goods.

"Their lawyer was in regular touch with Mack Walters. Turns out Mack was involved in my father's schemes. They made an agreement. Mack would draw a specified amount of money off the hidden account each year, and he wouldn't make a plea deal with the feds to turn evidence against my parents if he was ever charged. If Mack ever took more than his specified amount, my father would testify to Mack's part in the crimes they all committed." She paused for just a moment. "With the parole hearing coming up, Mack was supposed to speak on my father's behalf. It was perfect: a man who'd turned against my father, who claimed to be one of my father's victims, would now be willing to forgive him. My father was getting antsy with the hearing coming up, needing to communicate with Mack directly, and in I walk with a granddaughter whose email he can use."

Hudson didn't touch her, for which she was mostly thankful. Had he done so, she might have melted down.

As it was, she was thankful he was there, and no more than that.

She couldn't let herself fall in love with him again. She couldn't let the love inside her flourish. She couldn't afford the risk. It had taken way too long to fix what he'd broken inside her.

And with the secret she'd kept...he'd said he couldn't forgive her. She believed him. And she didn't blame him for that.

For leaving...maybe she did. Maybe it was time to own up to that.

As soon as Hope is found.

"My mom... When Hope went missing, my father tried to get an emergency meeting with his attorney, but we showed up first, and he knew we were going to see my mother. He sent a message through the delivery guy to my mom. It was supposed to be a strong message to just stay quiet. To let things play themselves out until he could get their attorney on it. The guy wasn't supposed to hold her wrists behind her back and shove her face into the wall..." She wanted to cry as she thought about her beautiful mother reduced to such a position, but she didn't. She just took it all in. Sat there with it.

"Mom's the one who told Jeanine everything this morning," she finished. Finished with that part of it, anyway.

"Wedbush got a confession out of Mack Walters, too," Hudson said. "When he heard he was a kidnapping suspect, he came clean. He copped to financial misdeeds from nearly twenty years ago, communicating with a federal prisoner through email and taking a yearly bribe to be quiet, but says that's all he's done."

Yeah, that's what she'd heard, too.

"It looks like none of this had anything to do with Hope's disappearance." There. She'd made herself process the words. Accepting them…she wasn't there yet.

"Walters has an airtight alibi for yesterday morning, and for last night when we were run off the road as well," Hudson continued, as though driving nails into her hands, pinning her to a situation she wasn't ready to accept. "And he was at the station this morning during the intruder scare."

She knew all of that. Liked the soft sound of Hudson's voice.

Still thankful he was there.

Even with no good news, he'd always been able to reassure her. Strengthen her.

"Walters swore he'd never hurt Hope or you. Apparently he's been watching out for you all these years. Making sure you were okay."

"He never helped me." She remembered that quite clearly and wasn't going to let him pretend otherwise just to get a lighter sentence. With the court or his own conscience.

"Because you didn't need him to," Hudson said, his tone gaining a bit more momentum. "Apparently Walters gave Wedbush a rundown of your successes. Said he'd expected to have to step in, but you'd done better on your own than you'd ever have done in cahoots with him."

She took the words with a grain of salt. How did you trust a liar?

"Jeanine said my mother begged for me to come see her." Her heart lurched as she brought up something she'd planned to keep quiet. She knew what it was like to be separated from your daughter. To not be able to do anything about that.

But the woman had deliberately lied to her, misled her all through the years.

"Are you going to?"

She hadn't decided. "I might. But I'm not going to visit my father again." That was a given. He hadn't been responsible for Hope's disappearance, but she didn't put it past him to have done so if it served him. Just like he'd used her email. The man served one god. It was green.

"And all the time wasted, looking into what he'd done...who knows where Hope is by now?"

"They never quit following the park lead, Manda."

But it wasn't getting them anywhere. Panic took her breath away, and she had to find her inner freezer again. She had to get inside. Wait for feelings to subside.

"They've been looking at security camera tapes from up and down the street last night. They'll get the vehicle. You just have to have faith."

Have to believe.

She looked over at him, let herself sink into that gaze just for a second, and she knew he was right.

"Thank you."

His chin stiffening, dimpling, he nodded.

And squeezed her hand.

He'd told her that he needed her.

It was a first. Maybe a last. But for however long she could help, she would be there for him.

Chapter 14

With the financial aspect of the case no longer relevant, and with another case coming in, Winchester flew out later that morning. But not before calling Hudson first. Making certain that he had everything under control. And getting his assurances that he'd keep the team updated on a real-time basis, not just the normal daily check-ins they all did on their group text message.

"You'll find her, my man," Win said as Hud stood by the couch he'd just vacated, still waiting for Mariah and Crosby to arrive with lunch. He hoped to God his friend was right.

"And when you do, Dad, you better bring her to the next board meeting. You know we're going to be all over her."

He grinned, as he knew his friend had meant him to do. Had a brief vision of himself in the plush Sierra's Web conference room in Scottsdale, with a petite blonde tech whiz standing beside him, and felt weak in the knees.

Probably something else Win had intended.

"What was that about?" Manda asked, her face looking more curious than stressed for a brief second. Looking more beautiful than she ever had.

And bearing almost no resemblance to the young girl he'd once known.

"What?" he asked, not wanting to share his brief mental moment with his daughter, with her. Hoarding it. She'd had years with Hope. He had a single, imaginary vision.

"Your smile…it was nice…"

Looking her straight in the eye, he aimed a blow. Knowing he was doing it and doing it anyway. "Win called me Dad," he said.

Her gaze dropped.

He was claiming what she'd taken from him.

Ten minutes after he'd told her they had to stick together, that they needed each other. Which he'd meant. And still meant.

But life wasn't that simple. Human beings weren't all just one thing, or one way. On the one hand, he and Amanda Smith were closer than ever. And on the other, they'd never be able to find common ground again.

At the moment, something else mattered more than any parts of their separate or collective selves. Their daughter mattered.

They had to find her.

She should have let her daughter take her cell phone to school. Hope had whined about it more than once.

She'd leave it in her locker as rules stipulated, she'd said. Had even mentioned once that she'd feel better having it in case of a school shooter or lockdown, so she could call Amanda. The girl could pull Amanda's strings, for sure.

But Amanda had been too aware of a presentation she'd attended at Hope's school, showing the hidden dangers to kids who spent too much time online. On the predators who would try to snare them.

And now, with no phone, Hope was missing.

She heard the car pull up and stood, heading to the front door and opening it before the bell rang. Maybe she should have let Hudson greet his friend, show her in, but the house was hers. She was the hostess.

And she knew that Hudson would just let her know, again, that he wasn't going to forgive her for robbing him of so many years of his daughter's life.

Just as she'd realized that she would probably never forgive him for running out on her. In all the fifteen years they'd been apart, he'd never once tried to contact her. Or provided a way for her to contact him. She'd had to go on the internet and look him up like some kind of stalker.

He'd had Sierra. All of his close college friends. He had his family.

She wasn't a part of it.

But his daughter would be.

The introductions were…unremarkable. With their hands filled with four boxed meals from a Mexican restaurant down the road, the two women followed directions to the table in the kitchen and unloaded, while Hudson delineated who was who, aloud. Amanda glanced at Mariah, met the woman's gaze briefly, said hello, and it was done.

There were more important things to focus on. Eating wasn't one of them, as far as Amanda was concerned. Mariah was an expert at profiling children, their needs, their emotional states, their probable reactions to various stimuli and their stressors. She was there specifically to speak with Amanda about her daughter and to look through all of Hope's things. To see how she kept her room, how she organized—or didn't—her things. To see what she liked, pulling out what appeared to be important to her. Even noticing what colors she favored. Jeanine had given Amanda the rundown on the phone. First she'd told her the news about her parents. The day had seemed like a lifetime to Amanda.

Mariah had already taken it upon herself to do up a flyer with Hope's picture and gave a stack of them to Amanda, saying officers were distributing them around key areas, including her neighborhood, Hope's school and the park where her tennis shoe had been found.

Amanda listened and finished over half her lunch. Remaining calm. Hospitable. If quiet.

As was Hudson.

Jeanine and Mariah handled the conversation for them. Mostly talking about the food. The people at the restaurant who'd taken care of them. The fact that a team of officers was canvassing the streets outside of Amanda's neighborhood, asking if anyone saw the black SUV that had been in the area the night before. They'd already been through her neighborhood asking about the man on foot that morning. There'd been some response, but nothing that had panned out into anything tangible yet.

Things were being done. Stuff was happening. She just had to be patient. To hold on.

How in the hell did a mother do that when her little girl had been missing overnight? When she was still gone and the main theory explaining her disappearance had just evaporated?

Angry with her parents for the wasted time, angry with them for their lies and deceit, and angry with Hudson, too, for hurting her in the first place, she got up from the table and put the remainder of her lunch in the fridge. On the shelf below the casserole she was planning to bake when Hope got home.

Anger was natural. She knew that.

But it didn't make living with it any more comfortable. By the time she'd rinsed her fork and put it in the dishwasher, Mariah, her long red curls falling around her, was standing at the kitchen archway, ready to get to work.

It was slow going at first, with Amanda standing around a lot, watching Hudson's friend go through all of her daughter's drawers, looking at journal entries, scanning a bulletin board filled with mementos of Hope's life, a concert ticket from when she was five and they went to see the stars of her favorite show on the well-known children's station. Amanda remembered how awestruck Hope had been. And how she'd sworn to Amanda that if she wanted to be a star too someday, she could be.

The kid had an old soul, as Amanda ended up telling Mariah. She talked about how Hope had first shown an interest in tennis when she was about four, and Amanda had bought her a little plastic kid's racket. The girl had never seemed to grow tired of it, to want to move on from it. Instead, she'd wanted to do more with it.

Hope was missing tennis practice that afternoon if she didn't get home soon.

Even if she did get home, she was going to miss it, Amanda amended the silent thought. When she got Hope back, she wasn't letting her out of the house ever again.

"Hudson loved you, you know." Mariah was sitting next to Amanda on Hope's bed, going through her tennis scrapbook. Amanda just turned the page, saying nothing.

"I don't know if he told you, but we met in this communications class. All of us on the board of Sierra's Web did. We were paired together, and topics got pretty intense. Everyone had to reach into their deepest selves and find a way to communicate what was there. To understand how difficult it was. To find ways through it. Ways to be most effective while still maintaining self..."

She stopped, and it wasn't until Amanda looked over at her that she continued. "Hudson's deepest place was you. He told us how he just walked out on you. After four years of being best friends, of being there for you, he just told you he was going, and the next day he was gone. He told us he never contacted you again."

Tears filled Amanda's eyes. She brushed them away. It didn't matter now. What he'd said then just didn't come into play.

"Then he fell in love with Sierra," Amanda said, standing. Leaving the book for Mariah to finish on her own. Leaning back against her daughter's desk, hands on either side of her, propping her up. Touching the wood that Hope had touched so many times.

The wood her daughter had complained about having to dust.

"He told you about her?" Mariah's green eyes held surprise. "Hudson never talks about Sierra."

She shrugged. "It's been a little intense here."

"He blames himself. We kind of all do."

She got that. She blamed herself for a lot of things, too. But blame didn't change things. Action did. Accountability did.

And she was accountable to her little girl, only, at the moment.

Maybe later, once Hope was back, she'd be accountable to Hudson. The concept seemed too far out of reach.

"Yes, but with them being a couple...I'm sure he thought he should have seen more...known more..."

He'd always been more aware than most. And had acted on that awareness.

"They weren't a couple."

Amanda glanced up at the words. Trying to remember exactly how Hudson had described their association.

"At least, I don't think they were," Mariah said, looking at Amanda. "I mean, Hudson has always been pretty reticent. And Sierra...well, it's pretty clear she was adept at keeping secrets from all of us...and I will say, over the years...Hudson's had a few relationships, but as soon as the woman starts asking about where the relationship is going, he's pretty much out of there."

Just as he'd been with Amanda. But not with Sierra.

He was dedicating his life to her memory. "He told me that she was his one healthy relationship."

Mariah shrugged. Thumbed through the rest of the book. Asked a couple more questions about Hope.

Then stood. "I think your daughter is building a good life for herself," she said. "She's determined. And independent. And by everything I see here, she plans to be around a long time. I don't get the sense that she ran away. At all. There's nothing to suggest that she's unhappy here. That she wants out. Her color choices... there's no darkness here. To the contrary, I think that home, family, the backbone that those things bring, are vitally important to her. You've done a good job."

The ice inside her melted in one huge puddle as tears sprang to her eyes. She tried to speak, but couldn't. Her lips trembled. Oh, God, how was she going to get through this?

"She's not a quitter, Amanda. You can be sure she's fighting with everything she has to get back to you."

"And she's smart." Amanda jumped as she heard Hudson's voice and saw him walk into the room. "I'm sorry, I was coming to tell you that Jeanine got a call on the SUV. They're bringing someone in to the police station, and she wants to be in on the interview. She'll be back for you in a bit..."

"I can come now," Mariah said. "I've got what I need from here. I'll give my report to Jeanine in the car and then head back to the airport myself." She walked to the door.

"I can't thank you enough for..." Hudson, standing only a few inches taller than the woman, was saying, but she cut him off.

"Don't," she said softly. "We don't do that. Don't owe each other. Ever…" She hugged him, he hugged her back, and Amanda had never felt so bereft in her life.

Standing there in her daughter's room without Hope there.

Her parents being liars and definitely no longer in line for parole.

Her child's father hugging another woman who was so close to him. Who bonded with him in a way Amanda never had.

Amanda was completely and utterly alone.

But she was still standing. The thought hit her hard. Instilling a surge of strength she'd thought completely depleted.

Just like the night Hudson had walked out on her. She'd thought she'd die that night. But morning had come, and she'd still been there, with a day to fill. And then another. She'd gotten through them.

"I meant what I said," Mariah was saying, looking from Hudson to Amanda as they left the room. "She'll be determined to find her way back to you. Just make sure that when she does, you're both ready for whatever comes next."

With Hope. Between them. Didn't matter.

She'd be ready. She'd take on any hardship.

As long as Hope is home.

Less than an hour after Jeanine and Mariah left, Hudson was back in the office, doing more deep dives on Hope's computer, looking at the house network, the router, anything that could show him activity that was unusual. Anything that shouldn't be there.

His team was looking for messages between Julie and Tabitha, looking for any clues about who the two people might be or where they'd come from. John was trying to hack into the back door of the website from which the messages had come. At that point, to save Hope, anything was a go.

Beyond cyberspace, someone had possibly been after Hudson and Amanda, the first time right as they'd come from the park the night before. What did they have that someone would want? Hope's computer?

And if a would-be intruder had been there that morning, did that mean he was keeping Hope nearby? And maybe other girls, too?

Not liking where that thought took him, especially in light of his thirteen-year-old daughter, he forced his mind to computer intricacies. Pulling it back again and again. Hope needed him to find whatever was there…

"Hudson!" Amanda came into the room, carrying what appeared at first glance to be a children's book.

"I found it!" she said. "I think I found it!" Coming over to him, she handed him the large hardcover book, open to two pages of large-type storytelling with pictures of a cat. "Mariah got so much out of looking at Hope's things and being in there…being close to her… Anyway, I started looking through her bookcase, thinking of the phases she went through, the different books she'd loved most, and remembered this…" She was talking so fast she stopped and took a deep breath.

It took him a second to read where she was pointing. *Tabitha.*

"One of my nannies used to read *The Tabitha Stories* to me and I, in turn, read them to Hope," she was saying, still talking at Mach speed. "They're about a little girl cat who's curious, always wanting to know about things... Hope loved those books. Because that's how she's always been, curious, needing to know... Tabitha. What if that's her?"

The fear in her gaze warred with hope. He saw both. Felt both in his gut, too, as he listened to her. Without a word, he brought up the website he'd been trying to get into the night before. Typed in *Tabitha* as the username, followed by Hope's usual password.

Nothing.

He tried the full name, *Tabitha Blake*.

And then all lowercase, the same.

"She sometimes signs her name *Hope S*," Amanda said.

He tried *TabithaB*, capping the first letter of each name as Hope had done on her regular username. Typed her password.

And...he got in.

He. Got. In.

Heart pumping, nervous as hell and ready to kick serious butt, he wiped his hands on the legs of his pants, told Amanda to call Jeanine and sat forward.

He probably wasn't going to like what he'd find.

But he had a feeling they were finally getting closer to Hope.

Chapter 15

"That's her!" Amanda burst forward, her hand on his shoulder as she leaned over to point at the profile picture associated with the account he'd just accessed. The little square photo had the same design around it as the partial picture of Julie they'd found the evening before.

Excitement burst through her for the second it took her to realize that finding her daughter on that site didn't bode well. Then panic set in, and she started to shake.

She read as Hudson clicked, finding the private message board that Julie Poppet and Tabitha Blake had been using.

He scrolled to the bottom first, but the most recent post was a week old and didn't say anything that would give clues to somewhere Hope might have been planning to go, or what she planned to do. Other than her homework and watching a movie with her mom that night.

She went on for a full paragraph about how great her mother was.

Which elicited envy and a "you're so lucky" from Julie Poppet.

Amanda didn't even realize she was crying again until Hudson's thumb wiped tears off her cheeks. He didn't say anything. Neither did she.

"If this is just a place where she talked to a girl her own age, then it might not have anything to do with her disappearance," she said as he scrolled up to the first message.

I couldn't believe it when my grandmother told me I had a cousin.

Amanda's fingers clutched Hudson's shoulder tighter as she read her daughter's first sentence. What?!

Your grandfather is her brother and they haven't talked in like forever because she disowned her family when she got married. She knew I was looking for family so she told me I had a family. She's really sad and misses your grandfather.

"Julie Poppet, or whatever her real name is, is Hope's cousin? My uncle's granddaughter?" She could hear the screech in her voice, but didn't even know herself if she was more scared or less with the revelation.

Shock was a given.

That was only the first paragraph and all that was

currently showing on the screen. Amanda took a breath. Straightened, tried to ease tension, but just felt it continuing to build. She didn't let go of Hudson's shoulder. He didn't shrug her off. Instead, he scrolled so they could read more, and she bent down to it.

My grandpa was the best. He died last year in an accident at work. He worked on roads…

How could she feel a pang for someone she'd never met? Family or not. The man had turned his back on a fourteen-year-old girl who'd lost everything…

They read more. Girl talk, mostly. About school. Boys. And then came something more serious.

From Julie, if that was even her real name,

The grandpa related to your grandmother was my dad's dad. My mom and dad are divorced and fight over me all the time. I'm only twelve so I'm not allowed to choose on my own where I want to be, which is with my grandma. My parents don't care about me. They're too busy fighting with each other and doing their own things. One time I snuck away and was gone overnight and neither of them even knew. I told them both that I was with the other and they never even checked to find out…

Amanda's heart sank. "She's a little younger than Hope, and in need…" She glanced at Hudson, his face below hers, but still only inches away. "Hope always fights for the underdog," she told him. "And more, she's always coming home with stories of kids in need and trying to figure out ways to help."

His lips pursed, he glanced from the screen to her, and then back. "You've taught her well."

"Yes, but what if she tried to take on this girl's parents?" Her own cousins, she realized. First cousins she'd never met. Hadn't even known about.

As dread filled every fiber of her being, she continued to read with him. Julie lived in Glendale, a suburb of Phoenix half an hour from Amanda's. Neither girl had pets. Both had cell phones.

Julie wrote at one point,

I wish we could see each other but I think it's good that we talk this way, though. I don't think my parents would notice who I talk to on my phone, but I'd die if your mom found out and stopped us from talking. If what you say is true and she blamed my grandpa for not taking her in when your grandparents were put in prison...

Oh, God.

Hudson looked up at her, covered her hand on his shoulder and gave it a squeeze, and then pulled her down to sit on his knee.

She shouldn't stay perched there. She knew that. And didn't give a damn.

You're so cool that you know so much about computers. I didn't even know there were sites where you could go just to have private secret talks... I can tell you everything and don't have to be afraid about someone finding out and getting in trouble. Or worse, pissing off my parents...

So they knew for sure that Hope was the one who'd found the dark web message site. They shared another glance, but Amanda didn't let herself linger in his dark-eyed gaze.

They quickly skimmed through more school stuff. Talk of tennis. And Julie's favorite pastime, reading. The girls talked equally about things they had in common and those that they didn't. Amanda and Hudson found the ponytail conversation interspersed with talk about jeans and leggings. As Hudson scrolled, two things became very clear. The girls talked every day. And they'd grown as close as sisters.

A post from Julie scrolled into view. Only two weeks old.

My parents have taken things to a whole new level of low. Mom's got a boyfriend who's a creep, and he walked in on me in my bedroom. He said he opened the wrong door, and left right away, but it gave me the creeps. I don't even think Mom likes him all that much, but she likes how much it pisses my dad off having him around. And my dad's with this bitch who doesn't like me. It's like she's jealous of me or something. The only time I'm happy anymore is when I'm with Grandma. Or talking to you. I'm so glad you found me. Please don't ever ever leave me...

Amanda looked at Hudson, who reached for his phone. "I have to call Wedbush," he said, and Amanda stood listening while he made the call. Wanted to sit back down with him again as he hung up a few moments later. But he didn't invite her back, and she knew she had to be strong on her own.

Still…longing grew inside her. Just to not have to do it all alone for a second or two.

She'd thought Hope told her everything. Would have bet her life on it. And instead, her daughter had had a secret relationship with her cousin for five months, and she hadn't known.

But then, Hope was her mother's daughter. And Amanda had been keeping a secret from Hope her entire life. She glanced at Hudson, sitting there working diligently, and so badly wanted to be able to give him to Hope.

And give Hope to him, too.

"They're searching Julie's real name now, going on the fact that she's Hope's cousin, and will do a welfare check on her…" Hudson said, going back to the message board for a second, but then bringing up screens of coding that made no sense to her. "Detective Wedbush has asked me to dig deeper into the message board these two used, to see if I can tell if anyone else was 'listening' in."

That was all he said, but Amanda's lunch started to churn dangerously. Someone else…he was looking for a predator…she knew it.

Could only imagine what the request was doing to him.

And she prayed harder than she'd ever prayed in her life.

Looking for perps on the internet was all in a day's work for Hudson. Over the years he'd been called on to help law enforcement many times in their searches for missing persons. And in their attempts to get evidence on suspected predators. He knew what was being asked of him. He knew what he could find, too.

And all of that knowledge ganged up on him, driving him hard to find anything on his daughter's computer that could possibly be there. He emailed John, who'd already been given remote access to Hope's computer, telling him specifically where to help look.

"It could be nothing," he said aloud, as much for his own benefit as Amanda's. She was behind him. He couldn't see her. But he could feel her there.

Needing him to give her a miracle.

Knowing he had no ability to do so. He could only give her the truth. It was all he'd ever been able to do.

His truth all those years ago had been that he needed to get away from her.

And now…

He might have to provide proof that their daughter was in serious trouble. A kind you didn't always come back from.

He hoped to God not.

"If this cousin is home…" His phone wasn't ringing, telling him so. It should only take a minute or two to trace Patricia Smythe's sister-in-law, to make a call…

"What if Hope went there? Maybe something happened and she went to help…"

Could be. He wasn't sure, since Hope hadn't been in touch overnight, that that would be a good thing. If the mother's boyfriend had found the two girls home alone…if Hope had tried to take him on on her own.

He kept typing, scrolling, clicking. Reading.

His phone rang. He had it up to his ear before the first peal ended. "Yeah." Amanda came into view. Perched on the edge of the desk beside his leg, facing him. Her arms across her stomach. Her long blond hair hanging down the sides of her face, but he could see the pinched worry there. The paleness.

He put the man on speakerphone.

"...name is Kelsey Bryant," Wedbush was saying. The grandmother wasn't picking up. Neither were the parents. The girl didn't attend either of the public schools they'd called close to her parents' residences. They were tracking down places of employment. Would let them know the second they heard anything...

Hudson put a hand on Amanda's knee. Just needed the contact. Needed to give her the contact.

"I'm sending over a photo of her," Wedbush continued. Looking at Amanda, Hudson nodded, trying to let her know that they'd get through this. She nodded back. He wasn't sure what she was telling him.

"And we identified the black SUV from last night," Wedbush continued. "Business on the corner turned over security tape this morning. Had the license plate. And when we told Mack Walters, who's now formally in custody, he admitted that the vehicle belonged to him."

Amanda's mouth opened, but no sound came out.

"Smythe's attorney had been in touch with Walters, warned him about your questions, and the fact that you'd been to see Patricia...she'd said you all only talked about Hope, and that she didn't say anything about the bank account, and they'd given her another warning not to do so, but they weren't taking any chances. The lawyer sent the text. Walters told his driver to send a clear warning to you as well. Instead, the guy tries to run you off the road. The driver's in custody for the moment, too. Said he figured that if you were involved, you'd get the warning, and if not, you'd think some idiot was texting and driving…he wasn't looking to get into the thug business."

"So why would he be lurking around this morning?" Amanda asked.

"He swears it wasn't him," Wedbush's voice came over the speakerphone and Hudson and Amanda shared a long look filled with mutual dread.

"And you believe him?" Hudson asked.

"Detective Crosby said that someone's on the way in with tape from one of your neighbors who just got home and saw the guy on her security camera. We'll see if we can positively ID him."

"It's possible that he belonged in the area for some reason," Amanda said. "The guy in the neighborhood, I mean. And it's possible that Hope's disappearance has nothing to do with Kelsey," she said. Hudson couldn't tell if she was hoping for that outcome or not.

It was pretty much hard to hope for anything at the moment, except for Hope's safe return.

Just that. Always that.

Wedbush agreed that both possibilities existed while the underlying fear he'd just heard in Amanda's voice rippled through Hudson with growing momentum.

As the call ended, he stood, took Amanda in his arms and held on tight.

* * *

When Amanda felt tears welling, she pulled away from Hudson, but not before placing a chaste kiss on his lips.

They weren't together—and they weren't going to be together. No way he was ever going to be able to forgive her for robbing him of the first thirteen years of his daughter's life. He'd never trust her.

And she didn't trust him with her heart, either.

She did trust him with Hope's, though. She hadn't. Not for a long time. But now that she'd seen him in action, she knew that he'd do his best to be there for Hope. At least enough to make her daughter feel loved.

And if he had to walk away, Amanda would be there to step in, to make certain that their daughter's needs were met.

They weren't together…and yet…they were something.

More than just biological components in a child's life. More than past friends.

While he went back to searching Hope's computer for hackers, with more of a chance of finding something now that the search was narrowed down to the one dark web message board site for the moment, Amanda continued reading emailed messages from the board Kelsey and Hope had shared. Hudson had sent them to her, and she was reading more thoroughly. Reading like a woman dying of thirst. Every word seeming to bring her a little closer to her daughter.

And to the second cousin she hadn't known she had. Kelsey reminded her a little bit of herself in some ways. A young girl who was lost and alone and scared, and just wanted to be loved.

Until she'd found Hud. And then she'd been happy for a while.

And Kelsey had found Hope.

Halfway through a message about a writing class at school—Kelsey's teacher was giving her all A's on her writing assignments and the girl was pretty sure the teacher wasn't even reading what she was writing— Amanda sat up straight.

"Kelsey goes to a school halfway between her parents' places," she said. "It's a charter middle school, and other than her writing teacher, she loves it, except that she doesn't live near any of the kids in her classes, but they all live close to each other."

As she pulled her phone out of her shirt pocket and dialed Jeanine Crosby, the approving look in Hudson's eyes lit her up inside.

Jeanine took the school name quickly. Assured Amanda that it shouldn't take long to find the school, with the parameters they now had, and for the police to make an official welfare check call. In a matter of minutes, if they could just find Kelsey, she might be able to tell them something that could help them find Hope. Jeanine promised to be in touch as soon as they knew anything.

Hanging up, Amanda couldn't imagine anyplace Hope might be that didn't involve her being hurt or in danger, or both, but she'd never have imagined her daughter carrying on a secret relationship behind her back for months, either.

Or what if…had the others already thought of it…

"Kelsey might not be who she's really talking to," Amanda blurted. She thought back to that class she'd attended on digital safety for kids. "Predators pose as kids to get to kids. I mean, I believed it was my second cousin. I believed what Kelsey was telling her, but what if this is really more to do with my parents somehow? I mean, think about it…" She paced as she talked, glancing at Hudson and then away. "The communication starts right after we visited my folks for the first time. And my dad hacked her email at the same time. This could all be part of it. They've got someone posing as Kelsey to get something out of Hope. They need to talk to Mack Walters again, and my parents, and…"

She walked back and forth, seeing only in her mind's eye, her daughter, her parents, cell bars and email accounts on computers and…

"Manda." Hud's voice beside her, his hand on her shoulder, had her nearly jumping out of her skin. Until he moved so that he was directly facing her, a hand on each shoulder, looking her straight in the eye. "They're checking into every possibility. You need to trust them to do their jobs."

"But…" They'd asked Hudson to look for a predator. If there was one, she needed it to be someone involved with her parents. "If it's connected to them, maybe they won't hurt her. Wedbush said that everyone who's come clean so far has said no one was supposed to get hurt… they were just protecting the money so it would be there if my folks make parole next fall."

She had to hold on to the possibility that her daughter could be home safe and sound before another night fell.

Before it got dark again.

His eyes continued to hold her gaze, steadying her.

And suddenly, she felt like she was steadying him, too. Because she wasn't in this one alone.

She was in it with Hudson.

Hope's father.

Chapter 16

"Hud, look…"

Hudson had been on a trail, fairly certain that it was leading him someplace that wasn't good, when Amanda's voice interrupted him. They'd been back at the computers about ten minutes, and he'd been aware of her every single second.

Knowing that if he found what he was searching for, it was going to be devastating to both of them. Knowing that John was looking, too, so if he was off his mark, John would back him up. If Hudson was on his mark, he'd find her first. He was that good.

But Amanda was interrupting him.

He glanced at her computer screen, saw a listing of phone numbers. "What am I looking at?" he asked, willing to look all day long if it helped her. But needing to get back to the trail on his own computer screen, too. They were approaching midafternoon. Limiting the number of hours they had left before darkness fell again.

"I just did a search on Hope's phone records. I can go back six months on my account online. She called this number in Glendale the day after we'd been to see my folks the first time. That must be when she told Kelsey to meet her on the message website. And when I did a search, there were no other calls to that number. There actually aren't that many, period, so I could scroll through pretty quickly..."

She was calm. Thinking. Doing what she could. And Hudson felt a surge of affection for her that shook him. Reminding him of earlier days.

Reminding him, too, of how he'd been in too deep and had had to run.

He couldn't fall for her again.

Couldn't hurt her like that again.

And yet, when they got Hope home, he was going to get to know his daughter.

Which meant he'd have to find some kind of workable relationship with Amanda. Something to consider when he could afford the time.

When we've found Hope.

He'd been about to suggest that she call the detectives and let them know what she'd discovered, but she was already doing so—even going so far as to suggest that they call that number, see if anyone answered...

The last almost made him grin, her tone of voice reminding him that in her regular life, Amanda headed up a team of top producers in her field. He trusted the detectives to understand that she was a mother hanging on by a thread and trying to focus, to help, so she didn't fall apart. Not a woman trying to tell them how to do their jobs.

He was glad that she was sitting there next to him. In fact, he was pretty sure he was better able to focus because of it—and didn't care to look into why that might be. Hudson delved back into the coding on his screen, working on an attempt to hack into the back door of Hope's secret message board. It was the only way he was going to be able to tell who else might have done so. If anyone had done so.

It was the only way to tell if someone else was pretending to be Kelsey Bryant. To trace the IP address of the second user...

The encryptions he was finding himself up against told him that someone was there, hiding from him. Except that considering the way Hope's computer had been laced with encryptions that went nowhere and seemed more experimentation than having any real purpose, he could merely be solving another of his daughter's puzzles.

If he wasn't in a hurry to try to save her life, he might have been amused. And impressed.

He'd made it through three levels of encryption, and stopped.

"Messages have been erased," he said out loud. Amanda leaned over from the chair she'd positioned next to him, still reading messages he'd sent to her laptop, to look at his screen. The whiff of ocean breeze that accompanied her told him she was sweating.

Hard to believe that even now she was still using the same scent of deodorant, but there it was.

"Can you recover them?" she asked. He pulled himself away from any thought other than computer- and Hope-related.

And shook his head. Not wanting to disappoint her. Wishing he'd kept his mouth shut. He talked to himself sometimes while he worked. A lot of times.

Because ninety percent of the time, he worked alone in a room.

"No, but I can tell that they were all from this past week," he told her. Typing some more. Focusing. She watched for another few seconds and then returned to her work.

He missed the ocean scent.

Amanda's phone rang before she finished reading all of the posts. She was exhausted, buoyed by panic, and when she recognized Jeanine Crosby's number, she put the call on speakerphone.

"Kelsey Bryant is missing." The detective came right to the point. "We reached her grandmother, who was out playing bridge today. And we have spoken to both of her parents. She apparently told both her mom and dad that she was with the other, and no one checked up on her..."

Amanda looked at Hudson. She'd been looking at him since she'd answered the phone, as though the sight of him would hold her up if the news was unbearable. He nodded. So did she. Not an affirmative. Just an *I'm here*.

"She made mention of that happening another time," Amanda told the detective, forcing air in and out of lungs encased in a too-tight chest. "On the message board."

"I know," Jeanine said. "Hudson sent the messages to us. We've got a detective reading them all."

Of course they did. But she was relieved to hear the news. She hadn't quite trusted anyone to do their jobs. To be there for her one hundred percent.

Which was why she was consumed with doing all that she could for her daughter, and why she was struggling that there was so little she *could* do, and...

"What about a phone? Surely, with co-parenting, she has a phone..." They could trace it. They probably already were, and...

"She was grounded from her mobile technology night before last for snapping at her father's girlfriend. Her dad pays for her phone. She was due to get it back tonight, when she was supposed to be with them."

Dammit. It couldn't all be happening. Something had to go right.

"I've talked to your mother," the detective continued. "She'd had her lawyer look up her brother years ago. She made several attempts to get in touch with him, but he'd refused to communicate with her. Her attorney got her the phone numbers of her brother and Kelsey's parents. That's the number on your phone bill. Her mom's home phone."

Amanda didn't even have a landline anymore.

They weren't talking about the fact that both girls were missing. Amanda sensed that Jeanine was most likely giving her time to process while Wedbush and others were racing against the clock with their next moves.

She had to get out. Being in the house, just sitting there, without Hope...it was too much.

"We checked the bus stop near Kelsey's home," Jeanine continued. "The bus she usually takes to her grandmother's house. Kelsey boarded it yesterday morning. And she got off at the park where we found Hope's shoe."

Oh God. Oh God. Oh God.

Hudson shot over to her. Put an arm around her, shaking her until she looked at him. And then held her gaze with his own.

"So they're together," he said, sounding not completely grim.

"It looks like they might be." Jeanine's voice also sounded cautiously optimistic.

"And that's a good thing." Amanda caught up with them. "If they're together, they'll protect each other..."

If they could.

"We don't know much more than that at this point," Jeanine said. "But I wanted you to know. Also, when I spoke to Kelsey's mom, I told her about the messages regarding her boyfriend. She was adamant that the guy would never do anything to Kelsey, but also admitted that he was going to be home alone with Kelsey last night. She had an awards program to attend for work, and it was her night to have Kelsey. That's why she thought Kelsey was with her dad. It wasn't unusual for Kelsey to go to her dad's when her mom was going to be out in the evening."

But Kelsey was gone. Just like Hope.

The detective rang off then, saying she'd keep them apprised, and Amanda sat there, still staring at Hudson.

"Those erased messages... I'll bet Kelsey told Hope she was going to have to be home alone with the creep."

She teared up as she used Kelsey's word for her mother's boyfriend. "Hope wouldn't let that happen," she continued after a second. "She'd tell Kelsey to come to her."

He nodded. "I'm already there with you on that."

"Can we hope that they stayed away overnight, someplace safe, so that no one made Kelsey go back home until the night was over? I mean, clearly Kelsey's mom doesn't see the guy as a risk, so the girl isn't going to trust that any of the adults in her life are going to help her."

"He could also have told her that if she said anything to anyone, he'd hurt her. Or her mom." Hudson's tone was grim as he said the last, reminding Amanda that this wasn't his first horrible crime case. Probably wasn't even his fiftieth.

But it was the first involving his own daughter.

"Then why haven't they come home?" She asked the question that logically followed behind her premise.

He looked her right in the eye. "I have no good answer to that."

And neither did she.

No.

Everything in Hudson stilled…just…stopped…

He stared at the screen, reading the evidence, and…

Energy surged through him. Angry energy. Scared-out-of-his-wits energy. Needing-to-go-kill-someone energy.

"What?" Amanda's voice brought her into focus. Reminding him that she was in the room. And that she had to know…

He stared at her. Words didn't come.

"You made a strange sound," she said, slowly…her statement laced with a questioning tone.

How did you tell your ex-lover that the child you shared was…

That her baby girl had been…

He couldn't sit there on the information, and he couldn't let her hear it by way of the phone call he had to make.

"Someone's been eavesdropping on Kelsey and Hope. I've just finally gotten to the IP address. It's registered to a Burt Cummins."

He picked up his phone. Hit speed dial. Glanced away from Amanda as he gave Wedbush what he had, including an approximate location of the computer the man was using. The call took about fifteen seconds, and he had to hang up. To face the mother of his child. To help her. When he didn't even know how to help himself at the moment.

He'd done his job.

But he hadn't been able to give her what she'd so desperately wanted.

Turning toward her, his entire system in a state of flux unlike anything he'd ever known before, a mixture of shock and helpless fury, he was surprised to find her…not buckled over in the chair.

Sitting upright, she was typing. He glanced at her screen. And scooted over closer to her. Reading what she was bringing up on her search of the name Burt Cummins.

There were a few of them. Varying ages. She narrowed the search to the Phoenix valley. Still a number of them.

And she went to a site that showed criminals in the area. "A good real estate agent checks crimes in the area, delivers statistics to potential buyers," she was saying as though she was in the middle of a normal workday or something.

The name Burt Cummins showed up on that site, too. Twice. There was the guy who'd peed in a public park. And the one who'd been arrested three times for DUI.

"Burt Cummins is probably not his real name," Amanda said next, not in a chatty voice, but one filled with unnatural energy. "You know, like Julie and Tabitha..."

"I got it down to the IP address," he told her. "But yes, it could be registered to a bogus name." He'd been able to narrow the computer source down to a block radius. It hadn't been in the valley, but rather a small town just east of Phoenix.

Superstition Valley.

A desert town that existed as an oasis away from the world. A place where bad things could happen and most of the world would be none the wiser.

A town that drew people who didn't want to be found. And where residences, many of them of the mobile variety, were spread far enough apart that neighbors wouldn't know what was going on next door. It was a town that respected privacy, that had few laws, and where the number one rule was to live and let live.

He'd been there once.

He also had access to databases that Amanda couldn't access. He knew there was no Burt Cummins living in Superstition Valley. And also knew that the detectives would be able to pretty quickly find out everyone who lived or had businesses on the block in question.

"I have to get out there looking," Amanda said, standing quickly and reaching for her purse. "I can start at the park and just drive. If the girls are hiding someplace and Hope sees my car, she'll find a way to get my attention."

She was scared to death. And he understood her need to get moving on things. To be out in the field, so to speak. He'd never felt the urgency before, understanding that he was more valuable alone behind his desk. But this was different.

This was Hope.

And Manda. He went toward her, not sure what he was going to do when he reached her. It wasn't like he could stand in the doorway and block her way.

And he wasn't going to let her head out alone, either. They'd agreed. They were in that particular battle together.

The battle for Hope.

The police outside would try to stop her, too, but they couldn't keep her hostage in her home if she was determined to leave. And there was no doubt at that moment about the woman's determination.

As it turned out, what to do when he reached her was one problem he didn't have to solve. Her phone rang.

Shoving her purse strap up on her shoulder, the black bag resting half on her back and under her arm, she answered with speakerphone on.

"We've got an ID," Jeanine Crosby said. And Amanda, visibly drooping as though air had been let out of her, glanced at him. Hudson's job was clear to him. He took her hand. Held on.

"We did a search of the photo of this morning's lurker that came in from the neighbor's security camera, and cross-referenced it with names registered to residences in the block in Superstition Valley and made a positive identification. His real name is Kent Cummins. Obviously not the brightest bulb in the shed, using his real last name. He's in his late thirties and currently unemployed. He's got a couple of complaints filed against him for inappropriate conversations with minor girls, two different valley cities, but nothing that was enough to convict him."

It was the worst kind of news. The confirmation he'd been most dreading. Amanda seemed to lose her balance, and he steadied her. Using the feel of her hand in his to steady himself.

"We've got an all-points bulletin out on him now and will let you know when he's apprehended."

It didn't mean the girls would be found with him. He could be holding them somewhere. Or worse, he could have turned them over to someone else.

"Why, if he had the girls, would he be lurking in our neighborhood this morning?" Amanda asked, still hanging on tight. To him. And to the situation, too.

Hope's disappearance—and the deception around her parents—was taking a huge toll on Amanda. But it hadn't broken her. Yet.

"That's one of the questions we'll ask when we bring him in," Crosby said. A vague answer.

Hudson needed the real one. "It's possible he doesn't have them," he said. "Hope put her address up on the private message board for Kelsey. He'd know where she lived…"

"Again, at this point, we can only speculate," Crosby said, frustrating the hell out of him. But he understood, too, and offered his very sincere thanks as the detective rung off so she could get back to work.

Amanda dropped his hand and placed her phone in her purse, which she moved back to the table, turning to lean against it. "It's too much of a coincidence," she said, giving him a defensive glare. "That he'd be here the morning after Hope and Kelsey go missing? He has something to do with this."

He didn't disagree with her.

"So why would he be here this morning? What does that mean?"

She needed answers. He played along with her, trying to find some. "Maybe he was gauging to see how big a deal Hope's disappearance had caused. Seeing the cop car out front…he'd know he was in serious trouble." It was lame. So he gave her the truth. "It doesn't make much sense, Manda. I agree with you. He's got to be involved. And God only knows what he was after this morning. Maybe there's another girl in the neighborhood he also has his eyes on…even someone who Hope knows… As you said, she put her address on the message board. He could have been watching her for weeks. And who knows who else he saw?"

She was trembling visibly, but her chin stiffened as he spoke. She'd needed the truth. He couldn't give her that, but he could be honest about what he was thinking. What ten years in his business, working on a lot of crimes, among other things, had taught him.

When he fell silent, she nodded for a good thirty seconds, then met his gaze again, and tears filled her eyes.

Not thinking, just acting, Hudson reached for her, pulled her up against him and held on tight, comforted by the slim, feminine arms that slid around him.

"We'll get through this," he promised her. "We'll get Hope through this."

But even as he said the words, he knew that they'd mean little to Amanda. He'd made promises in the past too. He'd promised to always be there for her. To be her safe harbor in the storm. And later, when they'd made love, he'd whispered something about her always having his love.

He'd made a lot of great promises.

And he'd broken every one of them.

Chapter 17

Amanda was going to Superstition Valley. Nothing would keep her from trying to find her daughter.

Shaking so much she was dizzy with it, she stood up. Straightened her shoulders. And her backbone.

"I have to go," she announced. He could come or not. But she was leaving.

"Where, Manda? To do what?" His conciliatory tone irritated her. She knew he was trying to help, but she'd quit letting him lead her a decade and a half ago.

Although he was there because she'd called him to help.

And she absolutely didn't want him to leave. Not with Hope still out there.

"I'm going to Superstition Valley to find my daughter." When he told her that the detectives wouldn't want her interfering in their investigation, she told him that she didn't intend to.

"I'm not going to accuse anyone of anything," she said. "I'm going to be on the ground looking for my daughter and Kelsey. Showing their pictures around. Someone, somewhere, has to have seen them. I can't sit here and let darkness fall around me a second time. I will be out there in it, searching for both of them."

There just was no compromise on that. A perv was involved in her daughter's disappearance. All bets were off.

"Are you open to having a search companion?" Hudson's words didn't surprise her as much as they probably should have.

Maybe she'd known he wouldn't let her go alone.

Maybe knowing that had given her strength.

Either way, she was going.

"I'm done with what I can do here," he told her. "John will continue to take apart Hope's hard drive and report in if he finds anything, but we know who she's with, and we know who was after her…"

Yeah, so? She looked over at him. And then said, "Please, come with me?"

He grabbed his keys. She grabbed her purse. The stack of flyers Mariah had left. And some bottles of water.

"We have no gun. Very little protection." He was the one who worked regularly with law enforcement. The warning was valid.

"We have instincts and a stronger will than anyone else to rescue our daughter," she countered as they headed out the door. Her parents hadn't protected her. She had to do all she could to protect Hope.

"I can go," he said. "What good will you be to her if you're hurt? Or worse?"

"What good am I to her if I'm not out there trying to save her from whatever is happening to her? My life isn't more important than hers, Hud. It's less." A key difference between her and her parents. And maybe the difference between the Amanda before Hope and the Amanda afterward.

The officers out front, a changing crew every shift, got out of the car parked across the street and came toward them as they exited the house. In two quick sentences, Hudson had them nodding and heading back to their car. And then, belted into his front seat, he dialed Wedbush, letting the detective know they were driving around for a bit and distributing some flyers.

"He said the officers would remain outside the house, at least until Cummins is in custody," he told her. And then added, "He also said to stay close. If they get Hope, she's going to need you to be right there."

She'd actually already thought of that one. "Superstition Valley is only half an hour outside the city. And if this jerk has her, that's most likely where she'll be. If she has to go to the hospital, it will be out there, and I'll be able to get to her more quickly."

She wasn't backing down. Her bear cub was in danger. Nothing else mattered. And if a miracle happened, and Hope made it home while she was away, then the officers would be there, and she'd call Mabel to sit with her until she got there. And if they left, it would only be because Cummins had been apprehended, and then she'd call Mabel to cover the house until she was reunited with Hope.

With one of those long looks that she'd begun to crave again, Hudson nodded at her, and started the engine.

It didn't take them long to put up flyers around Superstition Valley's downtown area. It wasn't huge. A few streets with businesses ranging from medical and law to pets and flowers and a tobacco place that also sold sundries and bread and milk. A couple of eateries. And bars. There were four bars. Two with pool tables. One with several expensive-looking motorcycles parked out front. And the fourth had a parking lot half-filled with pickup trucks that looked like they were used for work every day.

There was one gas station with a fairly sizable store attached, right off the highway.

There was no grocery store. Or laundromat, either. But ten minutes up the freeway from Superstition Valley was a much bigger town, a suburb of Phoenix, that contained anything anyone could ever need. From highrise fancy hotels to vegetable stands.

After he'd parked in the middle of the main street, they'd hung flyers on light posts without asking permission. He wasn't even sure if there was law enforcement in the town. From his research, it appeared that Superstition Valley was under county jurisdiction. There was no sheriff's office that he could see.

Which wasn't all that uncommon in the Arizona desert.

In the black pants, slip-ons and the button-down shirt he'd put on that morning, he stood out. But not nearly as much as Amanda did in her formfitting striped tunic thing, belted to show the perfect shape of her waist, and hanging to just past her thighs, making it very obvious, coupled with those leggings, that there were shapely hips beneath it.

Granted, neither one of them had planned, when they'd showered that morning, to be heading out to the desert. And taking the time to change when they'd found out that Hope could be out there hadn't been a priority.

When the third guy walked past and took a good long look up and down at Amanda, smiling at her and tipping his cowboy hat, Hudson realized just how much they were out of his element.

Hope was clearly in danger. And now it felt like Amanda could be, too.

He should have gotten that conceal-and-carry permit Winchester had talked to him about a while back. He was good with a gun. Just generally had no need to carry one.

He'd be rectifying that misassumption the first chance he got.

Amanda, seemingly oblivious to the attention they were getting, pulled open the door of a hair salon that had come into view. Inside, not bothering with platitudes, she explained they were from Chandler, their daughter had gone missing, and they had reason to believe she'd been in the vicinity. Just like that, all four women in the place were hovering over the picture she showed them. She added Kelsey's to the mix, saying the two girls were traveling alone.

All four women, ranging in age from twentysomething to over fifty, had looks of concern, of sympathy.

Their tones were filled with the sorrow they expressed as they told Amanda that they hadn't seen either girl.

"In a town this size, if they were here, we'd have seen them," the stylist said. "But we'll keep an eye out," she added, asking them to grab a piece of tape from a counter that served as a desk and tape the flyer to the wall by the door. "We'll be sure to call the number on the flyer if we see them." All four ladies wished them good luck.

And Amanda, seemingly undaunted, pushed on. They made it down a side street, back up to the main street, and Hudson stopped. Putting a hand out to Amanda to slow her down, too.

"Look," he said, pointing to a small hardware and tack store on the main road. "The flyers we put up. They're gone." He'd put two by the hardware store. On the lamppost and on a sign indicating the town name, too. As they moved slowly forward, he saw that none of the light posts had flyers.

"There's no sign of them," Amanda said, looking up and down the street as they came to the corner. She glanced in a trash can nearby. "They aren't in there, either," she said.

"Could be some kind of town ordinance disallowing signage, but for missing children, who were suspected to be in the area?" He looked up and down the street. It wasn't like there was a sheriff's office where they could go ask permission to post flyers.

Amanda pointed out other signage—one for a rodeo that had already happened. And then stepped forward. "So we go into all of the businesses, like we just did the salon. Ask if anyone has seen the girls and if we can leave flyers." She'd only taken a step or two when a loud crack hit the air not far from them. And glass to the right of Amanda's shoulder shattered.

A bullet?

Sweating, Hudson swung around, standing directly in front of Amanda, between her and the brick wall of the building, looking in the direction the shot would have come from, and saw nothing but a quiet, dusty old street with cracked pavement and broken sidewalk. Before he could turn back, a couple of men came running up, having burst out of the door of the closest bar.

"Come on," one of them said, ushering them inside. Heart pounding, on adrenaline overdrive, trusting no one, Hudson kept himself between Amanda and both of them. Between her and the street. And once inside the bar, he stopped in a corner and took her hand, making it clear, in his mind, that if anyone messed with her, they'd have to go through him. Keeping her sandwiched between him and the wall.

He could feel her trembling. "What just happened?" she said, close to his ear.

The better question was, what did they do next?

The men had gone back outside, joined by a couple of others—he wasn't sure why. Two more were behind the bar, and another sat at the end of it, looking at them.

Hudson pulled out his phone. Thought about 911, dialed Wedbush instead. The detective told them to stay put. Said he'd be there in less than a minute. He and Crosby were just leaving Kent Cummins's place.

There was still no sign of the perv. The quick theory was that Hudson and Amanda had pissed the guy off with their flyers. And, perhaps, brought him out of hiding.

The out-of-hiding part wasn't a bad thing. But it was time for him and Amanda to get to someplace safe and stay there. Preferably her house.

Amanda couldn't stop shaking. Couldn't stop hearing that loud crack. And couldn't stop thinking about two sweet, innocent girls being in the hands of someone who'd shoot at a woman standing on a street corner.

The fact that the bullet had probably been meant for her—and that she could be dead—didn't faze her nearly as much as knowing that the guy could have Hope holed up someplace. Nothing else mattered.

"I'm not leaving here without my daughter," she said to the three people blocking any view of her from the rest of the room. All she could see was the floor, the ceiling and them. Hudson. Wedbush and Jeanine Crosby, who had just entered.

"Do either of you recognize this man?" Jeanine held out a photo of a white man with sandy-brown hair, bangs covering most of his forehead, green eyes and a normal build. Average-looking. Both detectives were staring at her as though expecting some kind of reaction.

She shook her head. Hudson did, too. She knew who he was. Couldn't stop staring at the picture. "That's Kent Cummins?" she asked.

Jeanine nodded. Tucked the picture back inside her jacket pocket. But Amanda had a visual now. A face to go with a name. She knew who he was.

And she was going to find him.

"He can come after me, take me even, as long as he lets those girls go."

"Kelsey's grandmother is at the station in Chandler," Jeanine said. "Her parents are on their way there. Why don't you two go back and wait there?"

She shook her head. Looked the detective in the eye. "He's got my daughter," she enunciated succinctly, through gritted teeth, but didn't raise her voice.

"And if he didn't know who you were before, he does now," the detective said. "He's also made it clear that he won't hesitate to shoot you."

She knew that. Was trembling with the knowledge.

"And we don't think she's here," the woman finished. "We've already been inside several of the businesses, including this one, and no one's seen the girls."

"Maybe people here are in on it," she said. Not long ago, an entire ring of internet sex crime offenders had been apprehended in Phoenix.

"I'm with her." Hudson stepped closer to her. "For all we know, there's some kind of illegal business going on here. And there's got to be more we can do than just sit in a police station and wait."

Whether or not he'd told the detectives that Hope was his daughter, she didn't know, but his support meant everything to her right then.

Sirens sounded.

"If Cummins is in town, we'll have him soon," Wedbush said. "In the meantime, you need to get back to Chandler and let us do our jobs."

She glanced at Hudson. His gaze seemed to tell her to agree, without also saying that he agreed with the two law enforcement officials. Hoping she was reading him right, she nodded. Because she wanted the detectives back to work. And she needed to be free to do what she had to do.

She thought about the flyers and mentioned their sudden, mysterious disappearance. As she explained, both detectives stared at her.

"Someone will know who took them down." Jeanine moved them all toward the door. "Someone has to have seen him doing that. I have a hunch it's the same person who took a shot at you." She made a quick call, giving orders for deputies to start canvassing the area for the flyer stealer. To find out if it was Cummins.

"The FBI is working with us now, as well as the sheriff's office," Jeanine said. She didn't explain why, but Amanda knew. Internet crimes, child abduction and... more...would have elicited FBI response.

"This guy's either too smart for his own good, or he's been lucky up to this point," Jeanine continued. "But his luck is about to run out."

"It sounds like he might not be working with all of his lights on," Wedbush added. "Which means that you two need to get out of town now. You're a threat to his prize..."

The second he said the word, the detective stopped. "I'm sorry, ma'am," he said to her, sharing a sideways glance with Jeanine. Neither of them had yet admonished Hudson and Amanda for showing up in Superstition Valley at all.

"My car's right outside." Hudson stepped forward, heading toward the door, but Jeanine held them back.

"I'll have someone take you out to the gas station in

a different vehicle," she said. "And we'll get your car to you from there."

The door opened, and two of the men who'd run out came in. "No sign of anyone but cops out there," the bigger one said. "And Neil. He's not too happy about the hole shot through his shop window…"

Another officer arrived, ushering her and Hudson out the door and immediately into the back seat of a police car, shielding them from the road, before Amanda heard the rest of the conversation.

Once inside, Hudson handed off his keys to an officer who would follow with his car. It was all quick and efficient, and she felt as though eyes were peering at her from everywhere as they were driven out of town.

She didn't know about Hudson, but she didn't plan to go far. She'd go on foot if she had to. But she wasn't buying it yet that her daughter and Kelsey weren't nearby. Not in town—a guy didn't kidnap two girls and then hang around and shoot at people asking questions.

He didn't kidnap them and then lurk around their homes, either.

It didn't make sense to her.

She got that law enforcement had to collect their evidence, follow their leads. And their protocols. But she had something none of them had on this case.

She had mother's instinct. She was the only one out there with it.

And she wasn't going home without her daughter.

Chapter 18

Hudson was ready to blast mountains with his bare hands. His daughter was missing. Her mother had been shot at—or maybe the shots were meant for Hudson.

He wasn't trained, nor did he have credentials to bring the guy down. And he had no idea how to help. He'd done his job. His part was done.

And Hope isn't home.

The danger didn't bother him for himself. But seeing how close that bullet had come to Amanda…imagining what horrors Hope and Kelsey could be going through… made him weak in the knees. Something he'd never felt before.

Not even when they'd been searching for Sierra's killer. Sure, he'd been afraid for his friends with Sierra's killer gunning for them, but he'd never known even an inkling of the terror screaming through him now.

In the back seat of the cop car, he watched for flying bullets, as though he could catch one in midair to prevent it from hitting its target.

But Hudson wasn't a superhero.

He was the computer guy.

The one who walked when the emotional going got tough.

He shook his head to focus. Wishing he could just shove Amanda down to the floor and keep her there until the perp was caught, he tried to come up with a plan for as soon as they were on their own. What did Hope need from them?

And how was he going to keep Amanda safe while they figured it out?

How did you find two young girls out in the vastness of unending mountain and desert?

The internet was like a vast desert filled with mountain peaks and hidden caves. And he knew how to breach it. How to uncover what lurked there.

He was an expert at tracking that which wasn't meant to be found.

An expert at mastering that which most found impossibly overwhelming.

When it came to sticking around in the emotional quagmire of romantic love and expectation, he wasn't your guy.

But this...

Finding a needle in a haystack...yeah, that he could do.

The pep talk carried him into the gas station store with Amanda after they were dropped off and was still motivating him as his car arrived. He was going strong as she buckled herself into his front passenger seat. As he listened to her suggestion that they drive back to town, stay off the main road and search every other street there was, he was right there with her. It wasn't a big place. They could drive from one end to the other in a matter of minutes. Some of the roads led off to private properties. They could explore every one of them. And still be back in the city before dark.

"And we can see, maybe if we find people out, we can show them a flyer. Ask if they've seen the girls…"

That's how you found a needle in a haystack. You looked everywhere until you found something. Slow and methodical. Thorough.

He was her man again. For this one moment in time.

Starting the car, he talked about a side road he'd noticed on the way into town. Cops were everywhere, and he thought it best that they stay out of the way, lest they be more formally ushered back to the city.

Amanda agreed. Their gazes met, and they were as one again, with a shared mission. In the past, that mission had been survival. Getting to adulthood without parental love and emotional support.

Now the mission was finding the child they'd created upon a successful completion of the previous mission.

He put the car in gear. And in his peripheral vision noticed a man unlocking the driver's door of an older, though clean, pickup truck with a tonneau cover attached to the bed. The truck didn't snag his attention, nor did the hard plastic black cover over the back of it, though it was a nice enough one. What got him was the bangs.

Sandy brown and hanging low on the man's forehead.

"That's him!" Amanda's tone was soft, almost a whisper, yet filled with enough adrenaline to pump up the energy already shooting through him. He nodded, scooted just a little lower in his seat. "Do you have any lipstick in your purse?"

"Yes!" She reached for her bag. "Why? What are you going to do with it?"

"Nothing," he said, coming up with a plan as he went. "I want you to pull down the visor. There's a mirror there. Take your time putting on the lipstick. We have to see which way he goes, and I don't want to draw attention to us." He pulled out his phone, started scrolling, as though looking up something. "He saw us on the street, but hopefully he didn't pick out my car as unusual enough to put us in it," he continued, keeping the guy in sight as he hit speed dial.

The officers who'd dropped them off had sped out of the parking lot as soon as they'd handed him his keys, on their way back to help with the search in town. They'd probably get ripped for not waiting to see them safely to their car, or even out to the highway on-ramp.

It took three rings for Wedbush to pick up. His "yeah" blurted out over the car speaker system.

"We've got him in sight," he said, putting the running car in gear as reverse lights showed beneath the tailgate of the light blue truck he was watching.

"Where are you?"

"Still at the station." The truck backed up, then pulled forward, heading toward the exit. "He's in a light blue truck." He read off the license plate number. Watched as the truck turned right, toward the freeway, and then made an almost immediate left on a road that wound

quickly around a corner and out of sight. He was going
to lose him.

"All right, stay put. It's going out on the radio now."

"Too late." Hudson was already making the right
turn and preparing for the immediate left.

"What?" Wedbush asked, as Jeanine's voice came
over in the background, putting out a call for all available vehicles to head to the road immediately beyond
the gas station, repeating what Hudson had said. "Too
late for what?"

"We're following him," Hudson said. "No way I'm
letting this perv get away again." He hung up the phone.
Saw another vehicle, a dilapidated older car, make the
same left turn Cummins had made, and then followed
it. A car in between him and Cummins was a good
thing. Would make it harder for the perp to recognize
him behind the wheel.

If he even could. "He only saw us from behind," he
said aloud. Taking a quick glance, he saw Amanda sitting forward, peering ahead with her cheeks all pinched
and her eyes wide.

"There!" she said, just as he caught the clip of blue
metal in the sunshine, making another turn a quarter
of a mile ahead of them. This one to the right. And he
saw the makeshift on-ramp.

"He's heading to the highway," he said, tossing
Amanda his phone. "Speed dial one," he told her and
waited for Wedbush's voice to enter the car a second
time. Updating their whereabouts. Hearing again how he
could back down. State troopers would take it from there.

He wasn't backing anywhere. He hung up, and with
his foot pushing the pedal to the floor, Hudson entered

the busy freeway, weaving in and out of the cars that commuted regularly every day over the one hundred thirteen miles between Phoenix and Tucson. With that many miles of empty desert stretching between them and their destination, the speeds were sometimes track-worthy. He kept his car at eighty so that he could remain several vehicles behind Cummins.

"Do you think he's seen us?" Amanda asked, her gaze clearly pinning the man they were going to watch until he was in the custody of law enforcement.

He didn't think so. But wasn't sure. "We're blending in," he told her. And then added, "There's not much he can do about it, if he has. Not out here with all these vehicles."

A semitruck pulled in front of him, and Hudson quickly hit the brakes, pumping them enough that he wasn't rear-ended.

"Dammit! I can't see him!" Amanda cried out. "Can you see him?"

He couldn't, but, eyes on the road, behind him as well as in front, he watched his mirrors and pulled out into traffic. The pickup was nowhere to be seen...

"It's there!" Amanda said, pointing to her right. "He got off!"

The exit was so uneventful it wasn't even marked. Had to be some kind of service road. Crossing two lanes at once, Hudson drove through the median, scraping the bottom of his car all to hell, and re-entered the freeway on the other side, only to find there was no mirroring ramp on that side. Flooring the pedal again, he took a quick break between vehicles to cross back to the other side, and career off the freeway by way of the innocu-ous exit ramp.

His blood pumping hard, he glanced at Amanda, "You okay?" he asked. He'd thrown them both around a bit, but that's what seat belts were for, and they'd done their job.

"I'm fine. But I don't see him!" She wasn't crying, or even whining, but he heard the despair in her tone.

"It's not like this road has a lot of options," he told her, adrenaline pushing him. He'd been on many internet trails when he couldn't see the perp, when he'd had no idea where the trail was going to lead. All he had to do was keep following the trail, and Cummins would lead him to the answers they sought.

He knew that much.

"There he is!" Amanda's tone changed. He heard tears in her voice. "Oh, Hudson, we've still got him," she said.

"Call Wedbush," he told her, his tone sharp. He couldn't afford for her to need him right then. Not emotionally. Not if he was going to be focused enough to keep them both alive until they freed Hope and Kelsey.

He'd no sooner said the words than he was over a hill and faced with a bend in the road. Rounding it a bit too fast as he heard Wedbush pick up, he made the turn and saw the pickup just ahead. Too close.

He heard the shot fire almost simultaneously with realizing that the hood of his car had been hit. Saw a hand come out the driver's window of the truck a second time. "What's happening?" Wedbush's tone filled the car with alarm.

"Get down!" Hudson shouted to Amanda, and then, "He's firing at us," directed to the detective on the line. "We're on Mesa Road," Amanda said, her head almost touching Hudson's thigh as she lay across the seat she'd bared when she'd raised the console to do his bidding.

"We just passed a dry riverbed, about ten feet wide, with a marker sign that said Creote Creek…"

Impressed, glad she was on his team, Hudson didn't slow down as the other truck sped up. He wasn't going to lose the bastard. Amanda's hand slid up to his knee. Not with pressure. Just a presence that calmed him.

She was lying there, trusting him…

"A deputy is right behind you," Wedbush's voice exploded into the car. Hudson paid him no mind. Right behind him wasn't good enough. The road curved, and he leaned into the move as Amanda's head pressed against his hip. When the road straightened, Cummins had pulled away. Was a good six car lengths ahead of Hudson, but he made up time. Shortening the distance enough that if the man took any one of the little dirt drives into nowhere like they ones they'd passed, he'd know which one.

The gun showed again, and Hudson swerved to the opposite side of the road—a fatal move for sure if there'd been oncoming traffic. And was just getting back to his side to stay, after the shot missed the car, when he saw the lights flashing behind him.

Slowing down, he let the deputies pass him, but he didn't stop his pursuit. He was going to see the guy arrested. Know that he was in custody.

He and Amanda were going to be right there to find out where Hope and Kelsey were. To go get them. Or at least be present when the officers brought them out.

"We're going to get her," he said, easing back on his speed enough to keep Amanda safe in case there was more gunfire during the arrest. The guy was off his rocker enough that it could happen.

Amanda sat up enough to see out the windshield. He didn't like it. But knew he wouldn't be able to convince her to stay down. They wouldn't be Cummins's first target at the moment. He had bigger worries coming up on him.

"They could be in the back of that truck," she said, slowly easing to a full upright position, her hand sliding away from him.

Unbelievable that he missed it. And her head pressing against him.

And it dawned on him, as they passed a natural monument with a graveled visitor's pull-off, that he just plain missed Amanda. In his life.

He hadn't realized how much until he'd seen her again.

And pretty soon, he'd be out of her life again.

Except, not completely...

More sirens sounded, and suddenly, that deserted, dusty narrow desert road was crawling with activity as official cars coming from both directions trapped the light blue truck. Unfortunately, to Hudson's way of thinking, the man threw his gun out the window and came out with his hands up in the air.

"Too bad he didn't shoot one more time," he mumbled, half under his breath, his thumb pounding against the steering wheel.

"We need him alive, Hud, so he can tell us where Hope and Kelsey are."

He could be meeting his daughter in a matter of minutes. The thought of that, even in less traumatic circumstances, would have made him beyond jittery.

And they had no idea what they were going to find. If it was bad... His whole being ached for Amanda. It wasn't right, what was being asked of her. What could be right ahead for her to face.

He took her hand as they watched the scene unfold. As they waited. Wedbush and Crosby arrived, made their way through the swarm of vehicles. Cummins was nowhere in sight.

"They'll be questioning him here first," Hudson guessed. "First priority is going to be finding the girls. Getting them to safety…"

"What if they're in the back of the truck?" she said again. "No one's looking in the back of the truck.

"I imagine, with all of the sirens going off, they'd have made noise if they were back there," she added next.

If they were conscious. Still able to make noise. He didn't voice the thoughts. And before his brain took them any further, they watched as a deputy walked over to the back of the truck.

He heard Amanda gulp as both of her hands dug into his one, her nails biting his skin. He welcomed the sensation. It gave him something to focus on. Kept him grounded as he held his breath.

And…the tonneau cover was open and…the deputy shook his head. Hudson gulped in air.

"Okay." He quickly filled the silence in the car. "That's not a bad thing," he told her. "Chances were, if they were there, they wouldn't have been conscious."

So much for keeping the thoughts to himself, but the sunken look on Amanda's face, her eyes squinted in pain…

She was in emotional distress, and he had to help her. *I. Have. To. Help. Her.*

There it was. No fighting it.

Amanda was hurting, more than she could cope with. He knew it just by looking at her, and he had to help her.

It was a thing with him. Always had been.

"It might be a few minutes while they interrogate him," he said, watching as officers and deputies milled around, forming small groups and talking. Everyone was waiting. He figured Cummins was in a car, either the detectives' or an FBI vehicle. Being put on a very hot spot. They weren't going to spare the guy when it came to finding two young girls. "So...um...I was thinking...since we might be with Hope very soon... that we should talk."

No. That's not what he'd meant to say. He'd been looking for a way to distract her. Grasping, was more like it. Giving himself a mental shake, he sat there, feeling trapped.

And...kind of needing to talk.

"About what?" she asked.

He had nothing to give her on that score. Wasn't ready. Hadn't had any time to think, to process. He'd been too busy doing what he did best—losing himself in computer code. Following technical clues. Finding Hope.

Too busy to think about being Hope's father.

"I...have a right to be in Hope's life." He sounded so sure of himself. When he felt the furthest thing from sure about anything. Except that he had to be in his daughter's life. The sense didn't go away. Even with the words out there. Aloud.

And given to Amanda.

"Of course you do." Her response took his wind for

a second. It was so…anticlimactic. He'd been geared up for…he didn't know what.

But she was looking at him, not the jumbled scene in front of them. And her face had softened, right along with the big, blue-eyed gaze. Bathing him in an emotion so soft he had to build walls against it.

It was the only way he'd saved himself in the past. To erect those barriers that kept him on track. Facing forward. Making the most out of what he could do for himself, rather than focusing on what he *didn't* have.

What made him different from other kids at school, and later, as an adult. He had no wife, no parents, no siblings.

But he had a job in which he thrived. And the best, truest friends anyone ever had.

"I need your promise that you're going to be willing to work that out with me. To help ease me into her life. And to be accommodating when she and I come up with a plan."

He needed it clear that *Amanda* couldn't make the plan. Or even be a part of making it. That's not the way he worked. He wasn't a couple kind of guy.

That time was long gone.

"You have it," she said, glancing forward, but returning her gaze to him almost right away. "I knew the second I called you, Hud. I knew it would come to this. It's past time." Her soft tone melted through him, warming him in a way far more dangerous than sexual appeal would have been.

"She needs you, way more than I realized."

He'd been trying to mop up some of the goo inside him, and she shoved more in. Both hands on the steering wheel now, he clutched it so hard his knuckles were white.

"You're going to have to give up some control, and…" He didn't know what. He just needed to piss her off, get her on the defensive, hit a button that would shut off the compassion oozing out of her. "I won't have her in any kind of situation even a little bit like the one Kelsey is facing," he said then, holding that steering wheel for all he was worth. Coming up with nothing but the honesty inside him. "No using her to get at me. No using her, period. In terms of her, we're just good to each other. Good to *her*, first and foremost, always, but also good to each other. She can't be made to feel guilty, or worry about you home alone when she's with me. Which means you're going to have to get some kind of life…maybe take up tennis again. No, that's not good. She'd want to be there with you…"

"Hud." Her hand on his arm was a warning. When the back of her fingers lightly brushed his cheek, he shut up.

"You're right," she said. "About all of it."

He looked her way then. Wished he hadn't when he had the foolish idea that he should lean over and kiss her. "So…we'll figure it out." It was the best he had.

"Yeah, we'll figure it out."

And one thing was left. "When and how are we going to tell her?"

"I've been thinking about that a lot since we left for Superstition Valley," Amanda said. "I think we'll need to let the situation, and the state she's in, determine that for us."

Okay, fine. But… "How will I know?" He had to

keep her mind on a good outcome. Keep his own, there, too, lest fear for their daughter's safety eat them alive.

"I'm guessing the same way we've always known stuff," she said.

He shook his head. As far as he was concerned, they'd known nothing. They'd been kids winging it, and screwed up with their not knowing enough about anything.

"We look at each other, Hud. And we know."

Now she was talking nonsense. Next thing he knew, she'd be spouting all that soul mate crap she used to try to pin on him. Yeah, great, it sounded pretty, but life wasn't pretty. And believing in things that weren't there got you nowhere but let down.

When you were already as down as you could go.

"Like when they told us at the bar that we had to leave. You looked at me. We both nodded. And we both knew we weren't heading back to the police station to sit and wait."

Well, that. Yeah. "That one was obvious," he said.

"It's always obvious, Hud. And you do it as much as I do. You look at me and you know. And don't go getting all pale on me. I'm not a kid anymore, trying to pretend that we're somehow connected on a spiritual level. We just think a lot alike. We spent key formative years constantly in each other's company, growing up, discussing, learning. Because of that, we can read each other. So…when it comes to telling Hope, we'll look at each other and we'll know."

There was just enough logical justification in there to appease him. She'd probably done that on purpose, too. Didn't much matter. He'd managed to distract her long enough for Wedbush and Crosby to be heading toward them. Talking. Not smiling. But not wearing that sympathetic death look, either.

His plan to distract Amanda on the fly had worked.

He hoped to God he could come up with whatever distracton she'd need next.

Chapter 19

She couldn't just sit in the car and wait for the detectives to traverse the distance between them. "Let's go." She was already on her way out of the car as she said the words.

Shivering in her long tunic and leggings, in spite of the late-afternoon sun shining down upon the black pavement, Amanda walked beside Hudson, close enough that the backs of their hands kept touching.

Every step beat out a question from the repertoire consuming her mind.

Where was Hope? Was Kelsey with her? Were they okay? Was someone on their way to rescue them? Where was Hope? Was she okay? Was Kelsey with her? Was she okay? Could she see them? Had he hurt them? Were they okay? Close by? In Superstition Valley? Had she been close to them? Were they okay?

As they drew closer to the two with news, she searched their faces. It was as though everything else in the world faded. Hudson's hand touching hers, and the two faces approaching them. They weren't smiling. Not even a little bit.

Please, God, don't let them be dead. Please. Please. Please. The repertoire changed as the distance shortened. A couple of steps before they'd reached their destination, Hudson took her hand in his. She held on.

"He says he didn't take them," Jeanine said, her tone filled with warmth, was calm and professional, too.

Squeezing Hud's hand, Amanda refused the answer. "He was on her computer, and in our neighborhood this morning. He shot at us. Once we know for sure was him. The other time probably was, too. We know he was in town during the first attempt, because he was at the gas station shortly afterward."

The detectives nodded in unison. "He admits to being at the park," Wedbush spoke up, running a hand over his military-cut dark hair. "Says he went there to meet up with them, but when he saw them he changed his mind. He likes them too much, didn't want to scare them…"

She wanted so badly to believe that. And that put the girls back out in nowhere-land.

"He claims that he was in your neighborhood this morning just to try to verify that Hope made it home from the park okay, said he was hoping to see that Kelsey was there with you, but that, with the police car out front, he changed his mind and left." Jeanine's delivery held no clue as to what she was thinking.

"And you believe him?" Hudson asked.

"We're bringing his truck in," Wedbush said. "The forensic team will go over it, and we'll be holding Cummins while we check his alibis for the girls' disappearance, and then he'll be charged for the shooting…"

So…they really had nothing? Were no closer to finding Hope and Kelsey? Two days and everything had been wild-goose chases?

"We're going to need something of Hope's. A hairbrush, something with her DNA," Jeanine said, draining all sense of reality from Amanda's world. Her blood thinned, her skin heating, making her light-headed. "To compare against anything we might find in the truck."

Like blood?

"What was in the back of the truck?" Hudson's voice sounded beside her. She clung to the sound, to his presence. "Did you find blood?"

There, see, she'd told him. They knew what the other was thinking. He hadn't even needed to look her in the eye to get it. And without Hope, it didn't matter… They had to know what each other was thinking for co-parenting Hope. For telling her that Hudson was her father…

"There's no obvious sign of blood, no," Jeanine said. "This is just a precaution."

"We only got one set of prints off the tennis shoe in the park," Wedbush added, taking a step forward, as though eager to reassure her. "We didn't get a hit on them and are assuming they were Hope's, but they're still checking that. The lab wasn't able to pull any viable prints off the ripped photo. We might not have anything else to test. But time is of the essence, and if they do find anything in the truck, it will speed things up to have Hope's DNA on hand. We're getting Kelsey's, too."

What he said made sense. But her knees started to buckle. Hudson's arm went around her waist, and she leaned against him. Hope would be fine. She had to be.

Opening her purse, she pulled out the brush she carried there. "Hope and I share this," she said. "Take it. And we'll get you a brush from home, too."

Maybe forensics could use a shared brush. Maybe not. They took it. Thanked her. And as they said they'd be in touch, she let Hudson lead her back to her side of his car.

Hope needed her, and she wasn't going to let her daughter down.

But, just for a second or two, she'd allow herself to lean on Hudson.

Hudson was better when he had something to do. His mind raced to find something to do once they got Hope's hairbrush from home and delivered it to the police station. It would be dark in another couple of hours. Facing the darkness without Hope again…he was prepared to do that.

Things were supposed to get easier the more you experienced them. Not so on this one.

Starting the car, he waited his turn to do a U-turn and head back to the freeway and saw Amanda grab her phone. He listened while she asked her next-door neighbor to get Hope's hairbrush and deliver it to the Chandler police. Or to the officer outside her house if he was still there.

She wasn't going back. Which required a change in his plan of action, required a more immediate one.

IT work involved pursuing a lot of false leads. Trails that led off on tangents that didn't matter to the case. To dead ends. And he always went back to the initial finding, the concern, the clue, and started again. All roads led somewhere. Until he traveled every road, or found his target, he had to keep looking.

He'd already searched the dark web message site for any other boards Hope might have strayed to. There'd been none. Same for Kelsey. But that app...it linked the two girls. And it was where the two had made arrangements to meet. No one but Cummins had hacked into their board.

Just that one IP address.

Officers from the various agencies had been turning around in the road and speeding off. Cummins's truck was left. They still hadn't seen him exit the vehicle. He'd hoped to get Amanda out of there before that happened, but filled with new urgency, grabbed his phone instead.

"John, look at that message site for any other IP addresses coming from the Superstition Valley area. Or any other boards that Cummins might have been on."

"What are you thinking?" Amanda asked, color back in her face, but her expression still looking ghostlike.

"Just going back to the point of origin," he told her. "It's what I do."

"I know she's alive, Hud. I can feel it. I know that's woo woo, and you don't like that kind of stuff, but Hope is still alive."

And another option was that Amanda was unable to accept anything different. Either way, he wasn't giving up.

Or giving in.

"After they're all gone, I want to drive down this road farther," she said. "Cummins was going someplace. Think about it. He leaves town and comes out here...why?"

"Because he'd just shot at a pedestrian on the corner of Main Street and had to get out of town."

"But why here?" She spread her arm out in front of her, moving it in a semicircle to include the landscape around them. "He'd have a better shot of getting lost in Phoenix. Or heading southeast. Not sticking close to Superstition Valley."

"He could have been circling back to town."

"You think they're there?" she asked, her gaze meeting his directly for the first time since they'd exited the car.

"I don't know. I don't like that no one recognized them there. It's a bit far-fetched to think that the entire town would be in on hiding them. Even the ladies in the salon?"

"So why would he head back to town?"

"Maybe he has family there. Stands to reason that he'd have at least a friend. Maybe he was going to ask for help."

"There were a lot of other roads, closer routes, he could have taken to do that. He wouldn't even have needed to enter the freeway. Besides, he was at the gas pump. Unless he was completely on empty, that could mean he was planning to head somewhere farther than the few miles of Superstition Valley."

She'd always been good at analyzing situations. Used to seem like it was always to find a way to bring every situation back to herself. She'd taken everything so personally back then. Had been ultrasensitive. But back then, she'd had cause to be sensitive, he realized. Not only had her entire young world imploded into lies and court cases and imprisonment for her parents, but no one in that world, or any other, had come forward to care for her. Of course it had been about her. Of course she'd been paranoid. He didn't get the sense she was being paranoid now.

This more mature Amanda made sense.

Didn't mean she was right. He needed the puzzle pieces to fit one to the next.

A black car moved past with two suited men in the front. A suited man was seated with Cummins in the back. Wedbush and Crosby followed right behind them.

He saw her staring at the man who'd been spying on her daughter, who'd been in her neighborhood, who'd shot at her. She didn't look scared. She looked pissed.

"If he doesn't have the girls, why shoot at us?" she asked, saying nothing about the fact that the man had just passed by them.

"We put up the flyers. He was in the park. He panicked. Running down the street, taking them all down, that's a sign of panic."

She nodded. Was quiet for a moment. Then said, "Let's go down this road a little farther. Just to see if we can figure out where he might have been going..."

It was a plan. And he had nothing better.

Besides, if it would help Amanda hold on, while he figured out what to do next, he'd drive every road in the state. As many times as it took.

She had no idea what she was looking for. Fresh tire tracks? On gravel, how would you know? There were dirt road turnoffs, and pretty much all of them seemed to have fresh tracks to her. Hudson had put on music. Some instrumental new age jazz-type stuff. Nothing she'd ever listened to. But it was calming, and also engaging.

Since he had to concentrate on his driving, that left the responsibility of spotting their miracle mostly up to her. She took it on for all she was worth. She hardly blinked until her eyes got dry.

In some sense she felt as though her daughter was out there. Close by. But didn't trust herself to not be creating what she needed, so kept the perception to herself. Allowed it to comfort her some.

Clearly something bad had happened or Hope would have contacted her. She'd been gone thirty hours. Helping Kelsey out for the night wouldn't have required all day, too.

"If she's distraught, you know, depending on what we find…we might need to wait a bit before we tell her who you are," she blurted, the first words spoken between them in at least fifteen minutes. Out in the middle of nowhere, with only an occasional trailer set off in the desert to break up the terrain, silence didn't seem out of place.

Until he didn't respond to her statement. "I'm not going back on my promise to you, Hud. She needs to know who you are, for both of your sakes. But if she… if… She's a young girl, and if someone has mistreated her…we have to put her first."

"Always." He glanced her way and then back at the road, his gaze moving from one side to the other. They'd had the road entirely to themselves with the exception of one newish-looking red pickup truck turning onto a side road a couple of miles back. One of the gravel tracks that led to a trailer off in the far distance.

"And, just so you know, I intend to let you determine what's best for her up front," he said. "I don't know the first thing about parenting, and, like you, only want what's best for her."

It wasn't quite what he'd said earlier, but, knowing Hud as she did, she knew that both statements were true. He'd let her run the show until he didn't need her to anymore. And then he wasn't going to let her determine his course of action.

"You're a great mother, Manda. I trust your judgment." Not following how he got that, she swung her head to glance at him, caught a brief glimpse of his brown eyes as he turned to her, and accepted what he'd said. She'd told him a lot in the past thirty hours. He'd seen more, in their home, on Hope's computer.

And before Hope had disappeared, she'd felt like a good mother.

Her eyes trained back on the desert outside her window, she strained to see anything out of place. Anything that looked as though it had been disturbed recently. And fought tears.

Being a mother…it was the greatest gift she'd ever received. And the one thing that had shown her what life really was all about. What mattered most.

It definitely wasn't the money and prestige and power her parents had worshipped, that she'd been brought up to value.

And it wasn't the independence and emotional peace that Hudson seemed to treasure above all else, either.

Another ten miles and she didn't know where to go next. "How far out would he drive with them?" she asked. "He was in my neighborhood this morning. He'd need them somewhat close in order to get to Chandler early, right?"

She didn't want to think about what he'd done with the girls overnight. Horror-filled visions might turn out to be accurate, but they weren't going to help her be strong for Hope. They kept trying to torment her, continued to press at her consciousness every second, but she had to fight them. If they took over, they'd make her weak.

After they found Hope, then would be soon enough to deal with whatever reality they faced. And once Hope was home, Amanda would have the strength to deal with it. For Hope's sake.

That was one thing she could count on. One thing she knew for certain. If Hope needed it, she could find the strength.

"Let's see where this road leads," Hudson was saying. "If it's a dead end, we might find something there. If not, we'll know what it connects to…"

"Okay…" She liked the sound of that. Liked the smile he gave her, too. Not joy-filled, but…comforting. Offering encouragement. She shot some back at him.

Five minutes later of nothing but desert, his phone rang. She saw the name John come up on the car's phone system in his dash. He frowned, glanced at her—as though he wasn't sure he wanted her to hear what he was saying?—and then answered.

"There's another IP address registered to Superstition Valley accessing the same message site, Hudson. Guy's name is Hubert Grady. From what I can see, he's a couple of years older than Cummins..."

Hudson's gaze seemed glued to the road. He didn't look right or left. Didn't acknowledge her at all.

"Were they ever on the same message board within the site?" He seemed to assume that John would have checked before calling him.

"Once. A board being used by a pair of other girls, best friends who'd been separated when one's father was transferred..." John gave him the names.

"I'll have someone check to make sure they're both where they're supposed to be," Hudson said then. "Thanks, man. Great work." And he rang off. Dialed Wedbush immediately and gave the detective the news. Hudson's chin remained stiff as he repeated, verbatim, what he'd been told. His face like chiseled rock. Gaze still on the road.

Fighting his emotions.

Because he'd never learned how to deal with them.

Or just didn't want to deal with them. She watched him.

Analyzed.

Did he get yet that having Hope in his life meant taking on the emotional muck? Even when she was home and living a normal, healthy life, there would be muck.

Worries galore. Swells of love so powerful they swept you off your feet...

Watching him struggle, Amanda wanted to take the man in her arms and never let go. To ease his burden as he'd once eased hers.

To once again be a friend to him.

What she didn't want to do was accept the fact that

a second man could, at that moment, have her daughter and Kelsey.

Couldn't even seem to process the possibility. It was too surreal. Too much.

But the weight in her chest wouldn't let go of her, either. Wouldn't let her off the hook.

The nightmare just didn't end.

Chapter 20

Hudson kept driving as he talked to the detective. Just stayed on the road. He felt as though gifts were being taken away from him before he'd even had a chance to open them.

Pretty much his entire life he'd been on the outside looking in.

Since he hadn't been able to change his early circumstances, change who he was, what he'd come from, he'd opted to quit looking in.

He stared out the windshield, listened as the detective said they'd do a welfare check on the other two girls and would send someone to pick up Hubert Grady.

Was preparing to hang up, to figure out what to say to ease Amanda's distress, when the detective said, "They found a couple of blond hairs in the truck. Stuck in the latch of the tonneau cover. They're in the lab now, on a rush, being compared to hairs from the brush Amanda gave us."

"Does this mean you're keeping Cummins here?" he asked. At least give Amanda that much…

"Yes. We're going to hold off on the arrest until we get him talking, but we've got twenty-four hours before we need to formally charge him."

He pulled off to the side of the road. Listened while Wedbush told him they'd keep them informed and ended the call.

"They're someplace in or near Superstition Valley," Amanda said, staring straight ahead.

He nodded. Couldn't trust his voice to remain professional with her.

Didn't have any idea what to do with himself. His heart burned with rage. With fear. With a sadness he couldn't even comprehend.

He had a little girl, and he wasn't protecting her from the bogeymen. That was what daddies were for, protecting their little girls.

He hadn't been given that chance.

Maybe he hadn't earned that chance, either.

"What do you want to do?" he asked.

"Keep driving. Every road there is between here and Superstition Valley and back. I get that it's about a one percent chance we see something, but if we aren't out here trying, we don't even have that."

"I think we should turn around, though. We've come out far enough. I'll start taking side roads on the way back." He was staring out front. As was she. He needed the distance between them. Pulled out into the opposite lane and started the trek back.

"You think they'll get Cummins to break? Now that it looks like he has a partner?" He welcomed a question from her that he could manage.

"Depends on the dynamic," he said, "and which is dominant. What one might have on the other to keep him silent. And how confident they are that there won't be evidence to convict them. If Cummins really did leave the girls in the park, they could walk, and Grady hasn't done anything other than lurk on private message boards."

He slowed at the first crossing he came to. It amounted to a gravel turnoff. Which he took. And then, when he came to a gate, backed out of.

"It's possible that Grady had nothing to do with Hope and Kelsey. Might not even know about them," she said a few minutes later.

She was making his heart ache. He couldn't afford an aching heart. Wouldn't be as good to her, or Hope, if he went off on that tangent.

And absolutely couldn't start thinking about them as family. Biologically, yes. And Amanda...she wasn't going to stop caring. Being there for him. She didn't need him to be her partner for life.

And the three of them...no.

Sierra's Web, his friends, they were his family. The kind he could handle.

The kind he knew he wouldn't let down.

Or run from.

"I felt better when it was only Kent Cummins," she said after five more minutes and two more long driveways passed. "When I could pretend that being shot at was just a matter of him panicking. But with someone else involved…there could be more people out there who know about us. We were all over that town…"

"We can always go back to Chandler."

"I can't go back there. Can't face another night in that house. Not without her. And…there's a really good chance she's out here someplace, Hud. I need to be out here. To be close. It's like she can feel me here. Like she can draw on my strength and trust that I'll find her."

He wanted to shun the words as he had in the past. To put them down to her being a fanciful girl who'd led a cushy life and believed in fairy tales. He tried.

But the idea she'd raised, about Hope knowing she was close: he couldn't get rid of it. And without cell phones…a daughter's belief in her bond with her mother might be the only shot the girls had to feel any hope at all.

"It's going to be dark soon. We can't just stay out here all night." He'd need gas, for one thing. And it wasn't smart. On any level. He wanted to help Amanda cope, to help her do what she had to do, most particularly since it seemed to fit what he needed, too. But he also had to keep her safe.

He couldn't lose her, too, couldn't lose her again.

The thought hit him hard. Too. He hadn't been thinking of Hope or that she was lost.

Too. Just like he'd lost Sierra.

A friend he'd trusted with his life.

The idea settled on him. A friend he trusted with his life.

Maybe that was who Amanda could be.

Maybe that's who she'd been all along.

"Shouldn't they have called by now to tell us that Grady's in custody?"

They should have if… "It's possible he's on the run."

Her silence added to the grim atmosphere in the car.

"It's also possible he knows who we are," he reminded her. Darkness was going to be falling within the hour, increasing his unease keeping her out in the middle of nowhere with him, unarmed, with no training to protect her.

"What reason would he have for hurting us?"

He didn't know. But he didn't like the feeling growing stronger in him that he needed to get them to some sort of civilization. "People like that don't always act on reason."

"I can't go back to Chandler, Hud." He knew that tone. In the past it had always meant one thing. She'd made up her mind.

"There was a little motel on the exit between this road and Superstition Valley," he told her, not sure he was thinking smart, but liking the idea a whole lot better than being out on dark desert roads with her all night.

The thought of Hope and Kelsey out there in the pitch blackness…

Struck a terror in him that made him reach over and take Amanda's hand. "There was a diner attached," he said, forcing his mind to the motel. "We can get a room. Order dinner. Stay there just until we hear from Wedbush. And if Hope is indeed out here like you think, you'll be close by every minute."

And if the authorities found Hope close by…they'd be there.

He squeezed her hand. She squeezed his back.

And he headed toward the motel.

On a professional level, even a parenting level, they made a good team.

Maybe, down the road, that could lead back to the friendship he'd thrown away.

She didn't want to eat. Couldn't remember if they'd had lunch. But she ordered a chef's salad with a dinner roll because she was a mature woman, a mother with a child depending on her, not a kid who could afford to blow off common sense.

Hudson's stir-fry smelled good, too, and they ate seated at the small round table for two beneath the window of the generic motel room they'd rented.

Other than the table, the room had a long dresser, a coffee maker, a television and two beds.

Two beds. She'd heard him ask specifically for those and was glad.

Mostly.

If they ended up lying down, she'd have preferred to do so with him close by. And knew she couldn't afford to start thinking that way. The night before, waking to find him asleep on the chair just feet away from her... the warmth that had given her...was just something she had to file away.

Things were going to be difficult enough, even if, please, God, Hope came back to them unharmed, with Hudson being in their lives as Hope's father. No way it would be fair to Hope to complicate things further by having her mother pining for the guy. Hope would feel bad spending time with him when Amanda couldn't, feel bad talking about him in case it hurt Amanda…

The list went on. She chose to put it aside until she needed it.

With dinner finished, and the trash bagged up and set on the sidewalk outside the door as instructed, she listened as he called Wedbush and told him where they were.

Just in case. They'd both plugged in their phones as soon as they'd come in the door. He had a charger in his glove box. She always carried one in her purse.

Didn't surprise her that both of them showed up with essentials. They'd learned together how to take care of themselves. How to be prepared.

When he hung up, it seemed like a good time for her to bring up something that she might not get the chance to talk about again. Something that she needed to know if she was going to be accommodating and hands-off— and do it gracefully—when Hope entered his life.

Because Hope would be entering his life. She wasn't going to make it through the night if she didn't believe that.

And if Hope was pulling from her strength, as she imagined, her daughter wouldn't make it either unless Amanda found a way to remain strong.

"I told you I don't date, but we never really talked about you," she said. Well, they had, of course. Sierra had been his one healthy relationship. But that implied there'd been others. "Do you have a current girlfriend?"

"No."

He was scrolling on his phone.

"Come on, Hudson, you're a hunk, and young. You aren't going to convince me you don't see people."

Putting his phone on the table, the cord reaching to the wall beside them, he met her gaze head-on. As though taking her on.

"I see people," he said. "I don't have a girlfriend."

While the news thrilled her on a private, inappropriate level, it also saddened her. She didn't have a boyfriend, but she had Hope. She had her family.

He had…his family. Sierra's Web. In honor of the love he'd lost.

A pang grabbed her heart as fiercely as it had the first time she'd heard about Sierra and Mariah—the women who'd managed to do for Hudson what she'd been unable to do. It hurt not knowing what that… thing…was.

What about Sierra had created a place for her in his heart?

Amanda had given him every ounce of her. Heart. Mind. Soul.

And when he'd been free to leave, eighteen, graduated, with a place to go, he'd thrown her away without glancing back to see if she even made it to the trash bucket.

"So…these people…will Hope meet them?" She asked the question on purpose, putting it right out there on the table, because she needed him to know the reason for her questions wasn't personal to her.

Maybe she needed to establish the ground rules for herself, too.

"No."

"Why not?"

He frowned. And then his brow cleared. He moved, and she expected him to get up and walk away. Instead, he leaned forward, his arm on the table.

"I don't do relationships," he said quite succinctly. Making it clear the topic wasn't up for debate. "Not one-on-one partner relationships."

"Because of Sierra."

He shrugged. Frowned again. "I wouldn't say that."

"Why not?"

Shaking his head, he shrugged again, sat back. "Because Sierra wasn't… She was different…"

Yeah, she got that. Maybe he didn't get how much the other woman had shaped his life.

"I'm no good in relationships," he said. "You, of all people, should know that. I'm great in the beginning, perfect when it comes to being monogamous and supportive. And when things get emotionally engaged, as in, 'where is this relationship going' type engaged, I book."

Yeah, she of all people got that. And just out of curiosity, to pass another second without panicking about Hope out there in the dark, she asked, "How many others have there been?"

"That I walked out on?"

"Yeah."

"Three."

Wow. That many. Watching him, seeing the placid expression on his face, the acceptance, her heart cried for him.

And yet, he was happy with his life. Mariah had given that indication. So did Hudson, other than his completely understandable emotional quagmire with

Amanda. He was a guy who'd grown up independent. Emotionally alone, for the most part, from the time he was five until she'd met him at fourteen.

"I won't do it again," he told her. "Each time I convinced myself that it would be different. That I'd make it different. I'd work harder. I was going in expecting the emotional ties. I was ready for them. And each time, they strangled me, and I was gone. Leaving a trail of pain in my wake. Never again."

Each time. That meant her, too.

She'd strangled him emotionally?

Looking back, she could see that. He'd been her everything. And after everyone in her life had abandoned her, she'd needed to be *his* everything, too.

Something she'd been incapable of being.

He'd been alone for too long. Ultimately, alone was what he knew.

Maybe, if she'd seen that at the time…

But how could she have? He'd been all over her. As she had him. She hadn't sought him out. Quite the opposite. He'd always been there, waiting with open arms, for her to return to him. Wanting to hear about her day. Keeping her talking.

Probably so he hadn't had to talk about himself.

And as a spoiled, pampered and privileged little girl, she had been only too happy to soak up his attention.

And talk about every thought she'd ever had about everything.

Each time he vowed it would be different, he'd said. But…

"What about Sierra?" she asked softly. Because that

time he hadn't walked away. He was still loving her, living every day of his life in her memory.

"What about her?" He shrugged again, more easily, it seemed. Giving testimony to the fact that his relationship with Sierra had been healthy.

"You didn't walk away from her."

"We weren't a couple." He said the words as though everyone knew them.

She swallowed. Hard. Stared at him. "You weren't?"

"Of course not. I told you, she was my one healthy relationship."

"I thought that meant…"

"Sierra was like you," he said, elating her, and yet, leaving her afraid to hear more, too. "I could talk to her. Really talk to her. I trusted her with anything I needed to say."

That had been like her? Amanda?

That *had* been her. He'd told her all kinds of things. Not about deep-inside-him stuff. But so much. Even that he couldn't pass up his once-in-a-lifetime scholarship because he was afraid it would be his only chance to make something good of himself. To get ahead. To live his best life, rather than having to settle…

"But she was different, too. I wasn't attracted to her. Not in that way. She stayed just a friend…"

That which he left unsaid burned through her. If Amanda had stayed just a friend, would he still have left?

She knew the answer to that even before she'd finished the silent question.

He'd have gone. But he'd have stayed in touch. He'd have been back.

If I'd been just a friend.

If. A word denoting potential.

Except, *if* served no purpose in the world of her and Hudson.

They'd already crossed that bridge.

And burned it behind them.

Chapter 21

Wedbush called just after seven to tell them that Grady was still in the wind. And that Cummins had sworn to them, under every pressure and fear they'd placed on him, that Grady didn't have the girls. That he'd never had them.

His story changed on a couple of other topics. Cummins hadn't admitted to taking the kids, but his story changed a bit about where in the park he'd seen them. Where he'd left them.

About where he'd been all day yesterday, the night before. He hadn't stayed in town. His truck had been caught on a traffic camera showing him getting on the freeway.

But he hadn't swayed at all from his reason for being in Amanda's neighborhood that morning. He swore that he was looking to see if Hope was home.

Maybe because he wanted another shot at taking her, maybe not. No one had been able to lock him down on that part.

It was also clear, according to Wedbush, that Cummins and Grady were very close, had been best friends for most of their lives, that Grady was the smarter of the two, the dominant one, and that Cummins had done some dirty work for him in the past.

Cummins swore, though, that Grady didn't know about Hope and Kelsey. He'd known something was up, so Cummins showed him the private message board website, but not Hope's board.

Which fit with what John had found, so maybe it was the truth.

Hudson had been on his bed when the call came through, but as Wedbush continued to talk, his voice filling the room over speakerphone, he'd moved over to sit beside Amanda, who'd been propped up on her pillows, scrolling on her phone.

"Why is he in the wind, then?" Hudson asked.

"We'd like to know that as well. He wasn't at work today. Hasn't been home. Cummins guessed that maybe he was out looking for him. He'd found out that Cummins had had plans to get the girls and didn't believe him when he'd said he'd changed his mind. He figured Cummins was lying to him, too."

It was bizarre enough to be true. But...

"The hair in Cummins's truck..." Amanda said. "Why else would he have long blond hair caught in the tonneau cover of his truck if someone hadn't been back there, trying to get out?"

It was the first time she'd voiced the thought, putting the picture that he'd been carrying around in his mind into words.

"That's a good question," Wedbush said. "One we've asked. And one we need an answer for."

"Do you believe him about Grady not having them?" Hudson asked then. Over the years, he'd learned to trust the instincts of good cops, and Wedbush was definitely a good cop.

"At the moment, I do," he said. "He seems really confident on that part. At this point we're thinking that maybe he's hidden them someplace where he's certain Grady won't find them."

"So...it's somewhat safe to assume that wherever Cummins took the girls, with him in custody, they'll be scared and probably hungry, but...hopefully untouched for the night?" Had Amanda not been in the room, he'd have been a lot more to the point with the question.

"That's our hope."

Didn't mean they were right. Didn't mean the girls hadn't already been through hell or worse the night before. Didn't even mean they were still alive.

But for the moment...if their abductor was in custody...

"Look," Wedbush said, "with Grady still on the loose, and possibly knowing what you look like, who you are, we'd feel a whole lot better if you'd just go home and let us handle this."

It wasn't happening. He glanced at Amanda, got her confirmation of that. Neither of them said a word.

"If you won't go home, stay in your room," Wedbush said then. "We don't want to have to pull manpower from the search to get you two out of trouble. The watch is still on the Smith home. The neighbor is there for the night in case the girls find their way home?" He'd already filled Wedbush in on that plan.

"Yes," Amanda said. "And you'll call us as soon as you get the results back from the lab?"

"Yes."

"No matter what time it is?"

"You have my word on that, Ms. Smith."

"And I'm assuming that holds true in the event that Grady's brought in?"

"Absolutely."

That was it, then. Hudson left the side of Amanda's bed for his own.

Time to sit and wait. And wait. And wait.

Hope was okay. Spending the night cuddled up to her cousin for warmth. Probably scared. They wouldn't know their captor had been arrested. They'd be someplace safe from the natural elements. Coyotes, mountain lions. Thank God it wasn't scorpion or rattlesnake season.

The story built in Amanda's mind as she scrolled through various trails and local names for mountains and hills surrounding Superstition Valley. She was looking at blog posts from people who'd visited there, at state and county maps, at the online encyclopedia she trusted most and on social media.

Hope and Kelsey were out there someplace, and they were going to be found.

It was February and warm enough outside not to freeze. And not so hot that being outside for any extended length of time caused heat stroke or certain dehydration. Hope always had a couple of bottles of water in her backpack for tennis practice. And since her backpack hadn't been found, it was reasonable to believe that she still had it with her.

She didn't know what Kelsey might have. But figured she'd have had a backpack as well. Stood to reason, since she'd been supposed to appear as though she was going to school.

The jeans and T-shirt Hope had left in, the tennis shoes, would keep her warmer than leggings would have at night. And tennis shoes, her daughter's nimble feet were fully skilled in them. Hours on the court had ensured that.

She'd taken a picture of Kelsey's image from the flyers they were passing around, pasted it in a photo with Hope, and now had the two of them together on her home screen. Her lock screen. Her screen saver.

Hud had asked if she wanted the television on. She didn't. He didn't, either. He played soft music on his phone. It wasn't the best speaker system, but still, the sound was nice.

Calming.

He'd also called the motel desk and asked to have toiletry essentials delivered to the room. Had carefully checked the peephole before opening the door to receive them.

Everything was taken care of for the moment. Until they got Grady. Or knew about the hair DNA. On television it all looked so easy. Send it to the lab. Get the answer in a minute or two. Real life didn't work that way.

And she couldn't just sit there reading maps for the rest of the night. At some point, she was going to have to shut her eyes. Get a little bit of rest or she wouldn't have the physical strength to face the next day's challenges. A mother needed rest if she was going to move mountains.

"You ready for lights-out?" she asked Hudson just after nine. The phone could ring at any moment. They might be up and out of there, collecting Hope, taking her home.

Or…somewhere else. But until she knew different, in her mind, she was taking her home. One of their housemothers used to tell the girls in her dorm not to borrow trouble. Amanda hadn't really understood the big deal about it back then.

She did now. And had for years. Borrowing trouble didn't do anything but deplete your resources.

On top of the covers, she slid down to a mostly recumbent position, still propped on both pillows. The light went out.

"Try to get some sleep." Hudson's voice reached her in the darkness.

Five minutes passed. Every muscle in her body was tense. She was trying to relax them, one at a time. The jitters were just too determined to hang her up. "Would you mind if I turned on the bathroom light?" she asked. "Will the light bother you? I'll close the door most of the way."

"I don't mind at all."

Of course he didn't. He was Hudson. The perfect man when he was around. Truly, the perfect man. For her, at least.

She padded barefoot by his bed, tried not to focus on the shape of his legs, his shoulders, his butt, as he lay on his side, facing the door.

Flipping the bathroom switch, her gaze fell immediately on two toothbrushes, laid on one washcloth spread out on the Formica countertop. She and Hud sharing a bathroom for the first time ever.

The sight brought tears to her eyes, but she put them down to the stress, to missing Hope, to worry, as she quickly brushed them away and went back to bed.

Lying there, she tried not to move too much. To disturb him.

Or have him know that she was slowly climbing out of her skin.

She closed her eyes, tried to slide into the music he'd left softly playing, to let it take her away, but heard him move, turn over maybe, and her eyes popped wide open. She couldn't stop the buzzing inside her. And panic was building.

She knew the feeling. Felt it getting out of control. Just lying there…in the strange place…with Grady on the loose. Having been shot at, twice. She'd blown it off while it was happening, for the most part, as well as she could, because she'd been focused on finding Hope. Thinking that they were about to find her.

But with darkness consuming her, in a strange bed, so far from town, from a hospital…

Stop it. Get out of your head.

The admonishments helped for a second. And then the thoughts started all over again, until…

"Hud? You awake?" she finally asked, desperate to hold herself together.

He could call her needy. Think her all of the things she'd been back when he'd known her before. At the moment, what he thought of her didn't matter nearly as much as keeping it together so that she could be ready for whatever the morning might bring.

Have the inner strength and calm to give Hope whatever she needed.

"Yeah." His answer was slow in coming, but he sounded wide-awake. And just the sound of him...she felt stronger.

"I need you, Hud. I'm losing it over here."

"Yeah." She thought he was agreeing with her, but he didn't move. "I don't think that's a good idea."

"Please, Hud?" She had no pride. And not a whit of caring about propriety. She was riding on the edge.

"You know what will happen if I join you on that bed."

She'd had a thought or two about it. "I know how much better I'd feel right now with your arms around me."

His sigh was loud. And long. And then, in a wearier tone, "I'm not made of steel, Manda. And you know the effect you've always had on me."

She hadn't known for sure that it was still there...but thinking about it...distracted her. Warmed her. A lot.

"Would it be so terrible if we sought comfort in each other's arms? If we lost ourselves in another world for a bit? If nothing else, it might relax us enough to help us sleep."

She didn't really believe that part. But she was beyond caring. It was climb him or climb the walls.

"I'm never going to be in a relationship again, Manda. I told you that. I won't hurt you, or anyone else, that way another time."

"I know." Her tone held the honest conviction she

had on that matter. "Once Hope is home, we aren't going to be able to pursue anything anyway," she said, her gaze on the shadowed ceiling while her body rumbled in a different way. "Because we aren't going to make her adjustment messier by bringing our own emotional turmoil into the mix." And God, she was feeling emotional turmoil for him. All she could think about was Hudson's body. His hands on hers. Her own heat. The way her nipples were suddenly tingling. And it was good. So good. To be consumed by something other than debilitating fear.

And she was consumed. Way overboard. She got that. And didn't care.

Hudson was lying in bed in the same room as her. Their toothbrushes were side by side on one little white washcloth in the bathroom.

"It might help us if we get it out of our system," he said. And she flooded with moisture down below.

"Or at least, ease the need," she agreed. The curiosity. "Just to satisfy the question…"

She broke off as he sat up, a shadow in the darkness, and then she felt the mattress sink as he joined her. She didn't move over, didn't want to give him room to lie beside her. She wanted him on top of her.

"What question?" he asked, lying with one thigh between hers, and the other outside of hers on the mattress.

His face was just an inch or two away. She was mesmerized by the glint of his eyes. Whether it was moisture or reflected light from the bathroom, she didn't know. She just couldn't look away. "Will it be as good as adults as it was when we were just learning how to do it?" Breathless, she had little more than a whisper to give him.

"Ah, Manda, it's going to be so much better," he said just as his lips descended on hers.

Amanda gave herself up to the only thing powerful enough to take her away from the tragedy her life had become. From the soul-destroying fear consuming her. Hudson's lips were exactly the same as they devoured her mouth, making her lips wet. His taste completely familiar, she met him tongue for tongue, in the way they'd learned together. Found herself coming up with new ways to tangle with him. Without the shyness of youth, she brought the confident woman she'd become to the bed with her. And found a bold creature she hadn't known existed within her.

Getting out of their clothes was a slow and sexy process. An intense process. There was nothing fun or lighthearted about what they were doing. Instead, they were hot and breathless, making every second a burning lifetime.

"Your breasts have matured," he said as he pulled the tunic over her head and unhooked her bra, tearing that away to drop it on top of her tunic, somewhere behind him.

"Breastfeeding," she said, and then, with a hand around his neck, pulled his lips down to hers before she could follow the feeding thought any further. The only feeding she was going to be doing right then was on him.

The only one eating off of her was him.

He suckled her breasts, his lips on one nipple while his finger played with the other. She started in on the buttons to his shirt, and he stopped long enough to help, one-handed, continuing to tease her nipples with his other hand. Back and forth. Making her writhe with want.

With needing him.

His pants were off next, and the boxer briefs…she recognized the style on him. Was glad that something about him was the same.

His penis was larger than it had been all those years ago. Noticeably so.

"I didn't know this grew with a man," she said, running her hand up and down it as he'd taught her to do, paying particular attention to the tip, just as he liked it.

"Oh, God, Manda, it grows with you," he said, half groaning. "I'm not going to last," he warned. His voice sounded strangled, and she pulled him to her, spreading her legs, and rising up to meet him in one hard thrust. He filled her. So. Completely.

He froze as soon as he was inside her.

"Birth control," he wheezed.

But it was too late. As he moved to pull out, he came, releasing his seed inside her.

Chapter 22

Hudson and Amanda had sex twice more. Still without getting out the condom he always carried in his wallet. She'd just finished her period, she'd told him. Couldn't likely get pregnant. Besides, he'd already filled her.

It wasn't the idea of pregnancy that was bothering him nearly as much as the fact that he'd actually forgotten himself to the point of coming inside a woman without protection.

Even in the past, they'd used it. He'd never even considered the idea, back then, that he could have left her pregnant.

Obviously, he'd failed to take the condom off carefully enough. Or the rubber itself had failed.

Yet when he thought of the young woman who he felt as though he knew her deeply, but in reality had only seen in pictures, he couldn't really call the event a fail.

Still, he'd never, ever, ever come close to entering a woman without himself fully sheathed.

It was the extraordinary circumstances. He was almost able to sell himself on the explanation. Enough to stay right there on Amanda's bed with her as they settled into the sheets. He didn't hold her. They weren't lovers.

Weren't a couple.

But he lay there with her, flat on his back, staring at the ceiling, listening to her even breathing as she slept. As he had the night before.

He didn't figure he'd have the luxury of falling asleep. Still, after only a few hours in the chair the previous night, his body needed the rest...

He'd just rest his eyes for a second and...

Hudson sat straight up. The phone was ringing. His work phone. It was coming from farther off than the nightstand beside his bed.

The mattress moved beside him, and even before Amanda spoke, it all came rushing back to him.

"It's your phone, Hud."

Yeah, he knew that. Getting out of bed butt naked, he moved quickly to answer the call. Needing his pants on. Glancing at the clock.

Four in the morning. He hit the speakerphone button.

"Results came back from the lab," Wedbush said without preamble.

Amanda, standing right beside him, wearing her tunic already, handed him his pants.

"The hair was Hope's."

His gut rocked out. Amanda gasped, hiccuped and gathered clothes like a cyclone swirling the room.

"Cummins was more talkative when we hauled his ass off the cot in his cell and told him we had enough evidence on him to charge him with kidnapping and that the charges were going to escalate every second that those girls were still missing."

Hudson, gathering up the rest of his clothes, was already in briefs and fastening his pants.

"He did take the girls. Told them he'd kill Amanda if they didn't stay quiet and do as he said. He put them in the back of his truck, drove them out to a trailer on the road you followed him to yesterday. But Grady was there, and he didn't want Grady around them. He'd hurt them, according to Cummins. So he went inside to have a beer like it was nothing, and Grady was grilling him about the girls. He finally got him to believe that he'd left them in the park. Grady called him all kinds of names and told him he'd already found a buyer interested in them. So if Cummins didn't go back and get them, he'd be dead. Said the only reason he wasn't already dead was because Grady watched out for him."

"So he gave Grady the girls." Hudson couldn't take it anymore. Just had to know…

"No. He wanted some time with them himself first. To be kind to them. But when he went out to his truck to get them, they were gone."

"Grady took them?" Amanda's tone ended on a gulp and a high note. But she was standing. Her gaze filled with animalistic anger.

"We don't think so," Wedbush said. "There's been no sign of his vehicle, but we got a hit on his credit card at a gas station in west Phoenix hours earlier. Near Kelsey's house. She'd put the address on the message board. It's the only way he could have known who she was. We think he's out looking for them, and we need to find them before he does."

Amanda, hands shaking, helped him into his shirt. She didn't look at him.

The night was over. He couldn't comfort her.

"We're arranging a search party, setting up at Cummins's old trailer outside of town, to head out on foot at dawn. I'm assuming you two will want to be a part of it."

"Yes."

"Absolutely."

They spoke at the same time. Still didn't look at each other.

Which was fine with him.

It was all about Hope and Kelsey now.

They'd had their escape.

And it was done.

"It's the road where I saw that red pickup truck turn in yesterday!" Amanda's tone held a quivering, fear-filled excitement. "Oh my God, Hud, what if the red truck was Grady? What if he found them?"

The trailer, set back half a mile from the road, was old, with a window missing. The brown dirt, desert yard had rusty machinery and parts strewn around it.

"He was in Kelsey's neighborhood last night. That doesn't sound like he found them."

She didn't take offense at his terse tone. She understood the emotion driving it.

They were going to find the girls before darkness came again.

And they had no idea if they'd ever see them again. Or what state they'd be in.

For Hud…adding into the mix that he was searching for the daughter he'd never met…

"I'm so sorry," she said as they pulled into the line of already parked, mostly official-looking vehicles. Jeanine was in charge of the search and didn't seem to be there yet.

"For what?"

"Not telling you about her."

He nodded. Didn't say anything else.

She'd woken up feeling close to him again, like in the old days. In less than an hour, he'd managed to put more distance between them than there'd ever been.

He'd warned her.

She'd known.

It still hurt.

Way too much.

The man was not only the love of her life, he was her soul mate.

And the father of her child.

But as they got out of the car, saw Jeanine coming out of the center of a group of people with an electronic tablet in hand, all that mattered was finding Hope.

People were assigned to groups, and groups assigned to areas. Hudson knew as soon as he and Amanda set off with the other four people in their area that she wasn't going to stick to the path upon which they'd been told to walk.

Knew it even before she said, "Let's head this way," branching off from the others after only a few yards.

She'd started calling the girls' names, as instructed, with the first step she took.

Truth was, he didn't want her to do as she was told. He wanted her to know how to find Hope. Needed her to know. She knew their daughter better than anyone. If, as they now suspected, Hope and Kelsey had managed to get the tonneau cover open from the inside and get out of the truck, Amanda would know best where her daughter might head.

There was a science to search parties. Documentation, instructions and protocols. They served a good purpose and sometimes produced results.

And the search party would be out there, per guidelines, looking where and how science and past experience told them to look.

It wouldn't hurt to have Amanda following her own lead.

Calling the kids' names again and again, he adjusted the satchel on his back carrying the bottles of water they'd been given, along with energy bars for themselves and the girls, in the event they were the team that found them, in the event they were found at all.

"You think Hope would go this way?" he asked. Wanting to hear why. Wanting to know everything he could about the child. Finding her was upon them.

What would he say to her?

Would she like him?

Would she be alive?

Devastated?

"I have no idea," she said. "I just don't think it makes sense to have six people walking the same route."

It was so that they could be like a big blade being

pulled across the desert, covering all ground. In case there were bodies lying there that wouldn't be seen unless someone was directly upon them. So that they could see ground that might have been freshly dug.

Detective Crosby hadn't been vague as she'd given her instructions.

Amanda didn't hesitate, though, as she walked off to the northeast of them. She walked with purpose, seeming to belong out in the desert, in spite of yesterday's leggings, tunic and flats. She took on the land as though daring it to argue with her.

Calling loudly every other step.

She was fighting for her daughter's life. He knew that.

Admired the hell out of her.

Even as he needed to get away from the intense ties she wrapped around him. To break free and breathe without fear of loss.

The thought stopped him in his mental tracks while his feet forged on, parallel but to the left of Amanda—following instructions somewhat. Someone had to watch the ground for signs of fresh dirt.

Fear of loss.

Why on earth had he thought that?

Hell, he was all in with Hope, ready to camp on her doorstep for the rest of her life. To be there for her until after death. Even in the midst of the incredible fear that she could be lost to him.

So…fear of loss?

Made no sense.

They'd reached a hill, almost out of site of the trailer. The cars mere pinpoints glinting in the early-morning sun in the distance. Amanda didn't even hesitate before starting up it.

"You think they'd go up, rather than around?" he asked.

"They talked about hiking," she said, not the least bit out of breath as she kept up the steady pace with which she'd started. "On the message board. There was a whole day of talking about hiking. Hikes they'd both been on. Hikes wanted to take. It was all about going up. Seeing the world. Not just walking into nowhere. Kelsey's dad had taken her on a really cool hike up to the Flatiron in the Superstition Mountains. And the next week her mother, thinking she'd keep up with him, took her on what she'd said would be an even cooler hike, but it was all flat desert, looking at flowers..."

It was the most she'd said since they'd gotten out of bed. There'd been no talk of what had happened. No looking for it to carry any meaning into the future.

Hudson stepped up his pace. Continued calling to the two girls he'd never met.

He'd told Amanda the night could mean nothing outside the moment. And he'd been counting on her having Hope-specific insights into the search.

She was giving him exactly what he'd wanted.

Chills swept through her. Head to toe.

In between her calls for the girls, she'd heard a rock sliding. "Hud!" she called, her voice getting a little hoarse, as she turned toward the sound. The hill had become a steeper mountain, and the sound had come from off to the left, around a jutted-out piece of rock.

A cave?

Hope could have looked for one. They'd gone to cliff dwellings on a hike the previous summer, and Hope had talked all the way home about what life would have been like living in one. Had marveled at the strength it must have taken for women to raise children living in a cave on a mountain.

She told Hudson about it as they picked their way carefully through the rocky terrain. "The guide who was with us talked about how the cave afforded the residents a view that allowed them to know if a predator was approaching..."

Hope knew the caves existed all over the state. It made sense that she would find one.

She called louder and louder for the girls. Her hand was scraped from an earlier slide, her leggings dusty, but her insides were dancing with anticipation. If Hope and Kelsey were up that mountain, chances were, they'd be fine. Scared, certainly. Emotionally a mess, no doubt. But...untouched.

Mama's coming, baby. Mama's coming. The mantra repeated itself over and over in her mind as she took the last careful steps. She used to say the words aloud, rushing from her bed to Hope's crib when Hope cried out in the night.

She was around the corner and...

There was no cave.

No sign of anyone.

"I heard rocks moving, like someone stepping," she said, so crushed she was almost in tears.

"Probably an animal." Hudson was looking around them. Down the mountain and up above, too. "There doesn't seem to be anyone."

He kept walking and she followed him. The mountains were massive. Filled with flat terrain, steep climbs, dips and indentations. The girls could be anywhere.

And might not be up there at all.

Following closely behind Hudson, Amanda kept up the pace. Wiping impatiently at her tears.

He'd heard the rocks sliding, just as Amanda had. And twenty minutes later, Hudson heard a cough. It was muffled. As though someone had tried to stifle it. Camouflage it. He turned toward the sound, several yards behind and to the left of Amanda, around a rock formation, but on their same plateau, he thought.

Behind them.

On territory they'd already covered.

Putting a finger to his lips, he held Amanda's arm, glancing off in the direction of the sound.

Something wasn't right. Heart pounding, he listened.

If the girls were there, they'd have seen Amanda. Called out.

Unless they couldn't.

There'd been nothing beyond that formation but an unusually grassy flat piece of land. No sign of human habitation. And not likely to reach it without sound unless one was trying not to be heard.

Was someone following them?

It made no sense.

Unless it was some mountain man…a guy living off the grid. It wasn't unheard of in Arizona.

He might have seen the girls.

Could also have taken them.

And there Hudson was, alone with Amanda in an area

off the grid of the searchers. They remained still, as if in unison without words, and Hudson was reminded of her telling him that they'd know, just by looking into each other's eyes, what to do.

She'd been referring to telling Hope who he was, but she'd said it happened all the time.

He'd adamantly denied the assertion.

Maybe she'd been right.

"Let's keep moving," he whispered, angling his head toward the direction they'd been headed, not from the one they'd come. If someone was back there, and he was pretty much certain there was, he didn't want to be caught on the edge of a mountain peak if there was trouble. And maybe, if they could go a little higher, they could get a view of that ledge.

Five minutes later, they'd reached a larger patch of flatter ground. Large enough to build a house and have a garden. If one could get up there with goods to do so. And Hudson was certain they were being followed. He just didn't know why.

Pulling out his cell as he and Amanda caught their breath, he wasn't surprised to see that they had no service.

"We have to get down," he told her softly, his mouth close to her ear. He took a deep breath, inhaling the scent he remembered from kissing her there hours before, glad that they'd done what they had.

No matter what happened, he and Amanda had made love again. It had had to occur. He'd been thinking about it his entire adult life. The sex they'd shared. Needing to know if it had been as good as he'd remembered.

It hadn't been.

It had been better.

Taking her hand, he led her to a fairly steep incline, made up mostly of flat rock. They wouldn't be able to climb down it. But the area was behind a jagged ledge that would hide them from view as they made their descent.

"We can do it sitting down," Amanda whispered, dropping to her butt. Hands behind her, she started out. And just before Hudson dropped to join her, he got a glimpse of a man rounding the ledge they'd left fifty yards behind.

The guy had been turned to the side, paying attention to the difficult terrain. He'd dyed his hair, but from the photo Hudson had seen he had no doubt who it was.

Hubert Grady.

Chapter 23

"Why would Hubert Grady be following us?" Amanda's whispered question didn't hide her tension. Huddled together in a small cave at the bottom and to the side of the embankment they'd slid down, she didn't have time to think about dying.

If they were going to live, get to Hope, save Hope and Kelsey from the perverted man's clutches, they had to focus only on doing just that. Staying alive and getting to Hope.

"The only thing that makes sense is that he's following us to get to the girls." Hudson's tone, equally soft, was more intense than she'd ever heard. Like someone had shot him up with speed and it had all landed in his heart. "Like me, he figured you for the one who'd know what Hope would do…"

She glanced at him, sitting there, shoulder to shoulder and thigh to thigh with her. The day's worth of stubble growth on his cheek was a new thing, but she liked it on him. And his hair, he'd run a comb through it in the car, but it was still bed-tousled. Hers couldn't look much better. But long like it was, she could go a couple of days without washing it…

They'd brushed their teeth, at least.

Like me, he figured you for the one who'd know…

He had faith in her.

Never, ever had she known that small piece of information would give her the sense of value it suddenly did. Strengthening her. Filling her with a resolve she hadn't known was waiting in the wings for her to access.

"So, what do we do?" she asked. She might know some things about choices Hope would make. She knew nothing about criminal minds, not in real life. Hud might be the IT guy, but he'd worked a lot of cases with the police and FBI over the years.

"For the moment, we hang tight," he said. "We need to know if he saw us come down. I don't think he did. We were already sliding past where we could be seen from the top by the time those rocks slid down beside us."

Indicating that Grady had been just above them.

"He'll most likely think we continued on around and up." She agreed that the theory made sense. Her shoulder touching his, their thighs and knees touching…it felt right.

Destined. So they couldn't be a couple. So he took off when emotional entanglement got too deep. Didn't mean they couldn't be friends. Best friends, even.

Maybe even best friends who, down the road, had sex once in a while.

Or even, way down the road, best friends who got married, just for the convenience of it.

She was living the moment in a fantasy. She knew that. But, just like the night before, if it would get her through...

They'd sipped from their water. Her heart rate had slowed.

"We should keep going," she told him. "If he's after the girls, he's not going to do anything to us as long as he thinks we can take him to them."

"Which we can't do."

"Agreed."

"So our job is to keep on as though we were looking for them, but not go where you think they might be."

"Not find our daughter? No way."

He sat there, his eyes locked with hers.

"We get within cell range, call base, haul Grady in and then keep looking for Hope."

His smile, the first real smile she'd seen from him since they'd reunited, brought tears to her eyes.

It was time to go.

What he hadn't planned on was Grady catching up to them before they got into cell range. The man clearly knew the mountain far better than they did. For a while there, half an hour or more, he'd thought they'd lost the guy, that they could continue looking for Hope. That they had to continue looking and amp up their speed so that Grady didn't stumble upon her first.

And then they rounded a bend and the man was there... waiting for them, gun pointed straight at Amanda's head.

Something told him that if Grady shot, he wouldn't miss as Cummins had.

"Take me to them or I shoot," was all he said. Hudson watched him, but tried to take stock of the piece of ground they were on, too. Needing the full puzzle if he was going to find the piece that would set them free.

And then he gave Amanda a full-on look. She'd said they could tell what each other was thinking. He needed her to know that if they led the man to the girls, if they could even find the girls, she'd be a dead woman. Needing her to know that they had to continue with their plan.

What he read in her eyes, an odd kind of joy, completely confused him. Until he realized that with Grady there looking for the girls, they had just received confirmation that neither Cummins nor Grady had them. That, assuming they'd found a safe place to hide, they'd be okay.

Didn't seem to matter to her that her life was at stake.

That if she made one false move, the fiend holding a gun to her head could kill her.

And she'd never see their daughter again.

He'd never see her with their daughter.

He had to keep Amanda alive.

And they had to get to Hope and Kelsey. After two days out in the mountains, the girls were going to need food and drink soon, at the very least.

When she started to head back up the mountain, his heart sank. She wasn't continuing with their plan to head down to cell range so he could call for help. Just hitting speed dial on his phone and leaving it someplace would help. Wedbush would put a trace on the phone...

"Get up there with her," Grady ordered, still holding the gun on Amanda. He only had one weapon. It was two to one.

And the way Amanda had moved…that had put Grady in between them.

He didn't think. Didn't even see a puzzle. He saw a man who couldn't point a gun in two places at once. Making a dive through the air, he landed on the man just as Grady seemed to process what was happening. Turning his gun arm at the last minute, Grady shot.

Hudson heard Amanda scream. Felt the burn in his left hand, but on top of the man now, he rolled with him, reaching for the wrist of Grady's gun hand. Landing on his goal, he lifted the wrist and slammed it on the ground, again and again as they rolled.

"The edge!" Amanda screamed. He slammed one more time and the gun flew—right over the ledge that he and Grady were perched upon.

The look of evil anger in the man's dark eyes was unmistakable. Hudson was going over the edge on the next roll. Grady moved, taking Hudson with him. Unless he managed to hold on, the man was going to fling him over the edge of the mountain right along with the gun.

"Hudson!"

He wasn't going. He would not lose Amanda. And he wasn't about to leave her again.

Filled with fury, with desperation, he reared up, his fingers dug into Grady's beard and he slammed the man's head into the ground.

The ledge was grassy. He hadn't enough leverage to break Grady's neck.

But Hudson knocked him out.

Standing, wrapping his arms around a shaking and sobbing Amanda, Hudson took the KO for a win.

She was never going to be okay again. Never going to stop shaking. Never again going to feel relaxed or safe. Letting go of Hudson almost as soon as he'd grabbed her, Amanda used her teeth to rip into his shirttail and make a bandage for his hand.

"It's only a graze," he told her as they studied the damage together.

His fingers were all there. A small piece from the side of his palm was missing. But he was right. The bullet had grazed him rather than going through him. He still was bleeding profusely.

As though she'd had medical training, she wrapped him in the shirttail, putting on enough pressure to at least slow the bleeding, and tied a knot on the inside of his hand.

He watched her as she worked, and when she was done, she looked up at him, was startled to see something akin to happiness in his eyes. He kissed her then. She kissed him back, of course, but confused.

Startled.

Before she could question him, or even think, he grabbed her hand, heading straight down the mountain. They took as much of it on their backsides as they did upright, but the going down was much quicker than the uphill climb had been. Ten minutes after they'd left Grady passed out on the ledge, they had cell service.

Hudson had Wedbush on speakerphone almost immediately.

"Where are you two?" Wedbush's tone was urgent and filled with concern.

Hudson described their position. They were about a thousand feet above the cars, and from their vantage point could see them in the far distance. He told Wedbush what had happened. And where they could find Grady. Assuming he stayed passed out long enough for someone to get to him. He'd checked the man's pulse. It had been strong and steady. And there'd been no blood pooling on the ground around his head.

"We have a location on the girls," Wedbush burst out while Hudson was still describing the lack of blood pool. His good hand, holding the phone, started to shake. He stood at attention, holding it anyway, his gaze glued to Amanda's. Eyes wide, she looked about ready to come out of her skin with fear.

There'd be no pretending that everything was going to be all right if it wasn't.

"One of the teams heard them answering their calls," Wedbush continued with the same urgency filling his tone. This wasn't a *they're fine* announcement.

"From the best we can tell, they're about five hundred feet below you and to the left. On the ground looking up, I have no idea how they got there. Best plan is to go up and find a way down to them…"

"We're up," Amanda and Hudson said at the same time, still looking at each other.

"I know. Jeanine and I are with the team down below," he said. "Head west, listen for us, for them, and we'll call you if anything changes. You call us every five minutes to check in…"

The phone was already in Hudson's shirt pocket and they'd traveled several yards west by the time the man rang off.

She couldn't stop crying. Practically running, calling her daughter's and Kelsey's names in a voice gone partially hoarse, Amanda plowed through brush and slid on her butt, half aware of the scrapes and bruises she was acquiring, the rip in her leggings, and not caring at all.

Hudson, his bandaged hand showing blood through the shirt, led the way. The blood scared her. What they'd discover when they found the girls terrified her.

"They're calling out," Hudson said as they came to a ledge that required them to stop and figure out how to proceed. He wiped the tears from her face as he spoke. "That means they're alive."

He knew her fears.

He'd always known her fears.

"Do you think it went down like Cummins said?" she asked. "Do you think they got away before he touched them?"

If not, Amanda would keep her chin up and deal with it. She would have every ounce of strength her daughter needed to recover. But God… Hope was only thirteen.

"Grady better hope that's the way it went down, or I'll go back to him before he gets down off that mountain and kill him with my bare hands."

The words were shockingly brutal coming from Hudson.

But not from a parent.

It was only then that it started to really dawn on her she wasn't alone fighting Hope's battles anymore. Her daughter had a father who'd give up his life protecting her.

They'd gone another twenty minutes or so, without tears, and still making their every-five-minute phone calls, confirming that the girls were still responding to their names, before Amanda was certain she'd heard a faint sound in response to her own call. She stopped.

"Hope!" she screamed and looked over as Hudson's voice pealed at the exact same time.

"Mom!" Maybe that wasn't what flew faintly through the air, but it was what she heard.

"Over there," she said. Hudson nodded and started off in the direction from which the voice had come.

Down another steep embankment, she slipped, fell to her hip and slid several feet. She'd have a bad bruise. She didn't slow down a whit. Just stood up and kept going.

Calling. Listening to Hudson call. They were taking turns, giving their voices a rest. They'd both taken several sips of water, preserving most of what they had for the girls.

And then she heard it again. Faint but clear. "Mom! Mom! Oh my God, Mommy!" The last word was a scream so shrill it rent the mountains.

It was the last that did her in. Sobbing, she ran in the direction of the call. Ran. Down an embankment, across a flat piece of land, over a hill of rock, calling. "I'm coming, baby. Mama's coming!"

Down another slide, and she could see the cave. Like many of the ancient dwellings, it was barely accessible, dug into a flat rock face, but she'd been with Hope on the tour. She knew to look for the footholds. And to pray.

Wedbush and Crosby were both on the phone. Telling them to wait for someone to come lower them down on a rope, but she wasn't waiting. Hudson hadn't waited, either. He'd already found a foothold with a corresponding handhold. An ancient stone ladder.

Authorities could lower their ropes, bring their rescue helicopters, whatever they had to do, but she would be with her daughter, waiting for them.

Taking the "stairs" one at a time, slowly, Hudson hugged the wall, stepped down and then watched as she did the same. The ledge below was more than a ten-foot drop. If they fell, they might survive. She wasn't even fazed.

"Mom!" Hope's frantic voice broke her heart.

"Aunt Amanda!" She didn't recognize the term attached to her name, or the voice. And yet she loved it. So much.

Didn't respond. She had to concentrate on getting to them. On knowing that Hudson was getting to them.

And then, after two and a half days, and two even longer nights, she was on the ground, bracing as Hope threw herself at her, holding on for all she was worth.

"I knew you'd come. I knew you would." Hope's cries were muffled, but she heard them clearly. Savored them.

She couldn't breathe. Didn't care. Didn't know if her daughter was hurt. She just held on.

She was holding Hope.

Thank God.

Chapter 24

Hudson held the little blonde who'd wrapped her arms around his waist. Kelsey was tiny, several inches shorter than Hope and finer-boned. And she was sobbing.

He tried to offer comfort, while at the same time see if she was hurt.

And he couldn't help taking a long, painful look at the child he'd missed knowing for so long. Hope's hair was long, blond, thick like her mother's. In a ponytail that was matted. Her face was scrunched, mostly tucked in her mother's neck as she cried, but she was standing.

Kelsey was on one foot.

The other was held up and had a hoodie tied around it. They were in more of a gulley than a cave, but with a rock base above them, they'd had a ceiling of sorts. Two backpacks were laid together, like pillows, along the back of the gulley. There was a small pile of trash that included snack wrappers and empty water bottles, and a half-filled water bottle sat next to the two packs.

"Hope hurt her arm." Kelsey was the first to complete a coherent sentence. He sat down, pulling her down next to him, sheltered beneath his arm.

Hope and Amanda, they were in their own world. One that didn't include him. And they needed to be there. Amanda had borne his daughter on her own. She'd taken on the responsibility of two, while he'd run off to become something great, with others paying his way. The bond mother and daughter shared…it had kept Hope alive.

There was no doubt in his mind about that.

"It was her left arm," Kelsey was saying. "She hurt it when I fell on the last step getting in here. I hurt my ankle and she was catching me and we both fell…"

They'd been there a full minute and he'd failed to call Wedbush. Hitting speed dial, he held Kelsey up against him for warmth.

Reported their situation, giving a rundown of the injuries he knew of when Wedbush asked for them.

And heard that rescue crews, on the ground and, as a precaution, in helicopters, too, were on the way. If they couldn't get down on their own, they'd be lifted out.

Hope was going home.

He had to figure out quickly how to be the man— the father—worthy of her.

And hope her mother would forgive him for who he'd once been.

Amanda couldn't stop crying. Happy tears, mostly. Sitting in that gulley, resting against a rock, her daughter mostly snuggled with her head against Amanda's chest, she faced Hudson and Kelsey, listening as the girls took turns telling them about their abduction, their escape from the truck. She'd already checked out both Kelsey's ankle and Hope's arm, figuring the first for a sprain and the second, hopefully just a bad bruise. And she passed out snacks and water.

Hope had figured out how to unlatch the tonneau cover, but they knew they couldn't raise it much or their abductor would see them and come after them, which was how she caught her hair on the latch as they slid out the back. They'd hidden under the truck at first, until they could get a look at the area, and then they'd figured out together how to get to an area of cholla plants that would give them enough cover to head toward the mountain.

"Hope knew we had to find a cave," Kelsey said, smiling over at Hope and Amanda.

The girls were filthy, both with dirt and tearstained faces, but overall, they were okay. Really okay.

Amanda's tears were slower now, just an occasional drip from pooling eyes, but she smiled back at the little relative she'd never known she had. And vowed to herself, and a few minutes later aloud to both girls, that Kelsey would be family to them forever. That she was welcome in their home anytime she wanted to be there.

She'd yet to look at Hudson. Couldn't quite put Hope and him together in the same space. They'd been separate loves inside her for so long.

She just didn't know how to bridge the gap. Didn't know if she was meant to.

Finding Hope had been her endgame.

* * *

"So, you're what, an FBI agent?" Hope asked half an hour into their rescue. He'd hung up from Wedbush, who'd called to let them know that a professional rescue team was positioning up the mountain and would be scaling down to them with netted ropes to bring the girls out. It was the first time she'd really looked at him.

The first time he'd gazed into his daughter's eyes. "No," he said, feeling Amanda's gaze on him, but not looking at her. "I'm an IT specialist. I've taken over your computer, know everything that was on it, and I'd apologize, but it was how we found you."

She nodded. Seemed to take the invasion of her privacy completely on the chin. In spite of the fact that she'd know he knew about the diary he'd had access to. He and Amanda had both read it, and it hadn't amounted to anything to help with the case. But he knew that she hated having periods and thought they were gross.

"My name's Hudson," he said.

She nodded, a little sleepy-looking, and seemingly almost content now, as she half lay against her mother, her limp left arm lying across her stomach. And then she sat upright. Looked at her mom.

"Wait a minute," she said, her nose inches from Amanda's, her tone brooking no funny stuff. "Is this *the* Hudson? As in Hud?" she asked, then looked back at Hudson.

"I mean, it's an unusual name," she said, looking at him like everything was his fault. Which he'd come to realize, was mostly true.

He'd lost the first thirteen years of his daughter's life because he'd been a coward. Driving Amanda to be more while trying to take charge of his life and running from his own fear of loving and losing. Better to be on your own than to be five years old and stripped of everything…

"You are, aren't you?" Hope certainly had her mother's tenacity. She looked back at Amanda. "Is he *the* Hud?"

Wait a minute. *The* Hud? Everything stopped. He was a man in a cloud. Processing. Following the trail.

Hope knew his name? Knew about him?

"Yes, he's *the* Hud." Amanda's voice pulled him back. "I found out a while ago that he was a computer expert, and when you went missing, and they thought the key to finding you might be on your computer, I took a chance that he'd remember me, and I called him."

Hope's very open and demanding gaze turned back on him. "And you came," she said, smiling.

He was still trying to get together with the part that she knew his name.

"Mom talks about you a lot," she told him. "About how, when she was just a year older than me, she was taken from her home, lost everyone she ever knew, and how you became her friend at the children's home. You were like, saving her life. Over and over. You have no idea how many times I've heard, 'Hud would say…'"

She went on. He couldn't remember saying the specific things Amanda had quoted him on, but they sounded like things he'd tell her.

"Wait a minute." Kelsey sat up. "Am I getting that you two were friends in high school?" She looked to Amanda and then up at him.

Amanda nodded. So he did, too. Still not quite meeting her eyes.

She'd raised his daughter to know him. Teaching Hope through wisdom and comfort he'd somehow given Amanda.

He didn't know what to do with that.

How to accept it all.

"And Hope says you're only thirty-two. Not quite nineteen years older than her, which is a lot younger than my mom and dad." She was looking at Amanda now.

Uh-oh. Hudson looked at Amanda, too.

Look at me, dammit.

Instead, she was looking at Hope, who was shaking her head. "Hud was her friend before she left the home. I came after. Hud got this scholarship and moved to Arkansas, and then Mom left the home before he could get in touch with her, which is why they lost touch," Hope said. "And that was all before me..."

She looked at her mother for confirmation. Amanda's expectant expression didn't change, and Hope frowned. And then she pinned Hudson with a glare that was clearly accusatory. "How old were you when you left?"

"Eighteen."

"How old are you now?"

"Thirty-two."

She looked at her mother again. And then Hudson. Her eyes widened. With shock, not glee. No sign at all of happiness there.

"Holy crap!" She kept looking between the two of them, eyes wide, mouth open. "You got that great scholarship, and left and didn't get in touch with my mom... and...then she didn't try to find you, to tell you..." Her eyes filled with tears as she stared at him.

He looked at Amanda, who had eyes only for their daughter.

"Yeah, I'm your father, Hope. And no, I didn't know about you until yesterday. But it's not because your mom didn't tell me. Well, of course, it is that. I didn't know. But she couldn't tell me. I walked out on her."

The frown, the disappointment on that young face would be with him forever. "But why? You were so great, the best friend ever, and…why would you *do* that?"

He'd only get one chance. Even he could figure that one out.

"Because I was afraid," he told her. Honesty was all he had. "I'd lost my family so young, grew up in that home…and your mom…she was so beautiful, came from a privileged world I couldn't even imagine. I knew I wasn't good enough for her. Knew that when she got out, she'd find her way back to the life she'd been born into. No way ordinary was ever going to be good enough for her, and ordinary was all I'd ever be."

It all came pouring out. All of it. Things he hadn't told Sierra. Hadn't even told himself.

And when it lay there in the gulley, thickening the silence that had enveloped them, he looked at Amanda again.

This time she was looking back at him.

Straight in the eye.

And somehow, miraculously, he knew.

It had always been right there. All he had to do was be man enough, strong enough, to accept it.

"Will you marry me, Manda Smith? And let me spend the rest of my life loving you and our beautiful, strong and wiser-than-her-years daughter?"

Her smile rivaled any mother who had ever lived. Tears filled her eyes. She opened her mouth, and Hope's voice filled the air.

"Of course we say yes," she said. "But that doesn't mean it's all okay." She shivered, clearly favoring her left arm. It wasn't all okay. There'd be residual effects from the past couple of days—fears to combat, a trip to the hospital, and then tough months of getting to know each other, too. There'd be battles of wills, resentments, misunderstandings. And there'd be love.

He looked at her, at her mother, and back again, finding a piece of himself he'd lost as a kid. The piece that knew he was part of a family. A live-in, everyday, there-all-the-time, put-you-first family. None of it made him feel trapped. Because he finally understood that he was enough. He'd always been enough. It was him who'd found himself wanting. Himself he'd been running from.

"You have to stop using the same password for every site," he said then. Where the words came from, he didn't know, but there they were, landing on his daughter's shoulders. "And we're going to have a talk about ever visiting the dark web again."

"So, like, you're going to start bossing me around now? I don't even know you."

"That's what fathers do," he said right back to her. "And…I'll work on encryption technique with you. I can teach you anything you'd ever want to know about that."

"This is the coolest thing ever," Kelsey piped up beside them. She'd moved her leg, moaned and sat back against his side. Then said, "I can't wait to come spend the night at your house."

Their house. It would have to be Amanda's home. His condo wasn't a place to raise a family.

The thought brought another to mind.

He and Amanda were still young. Could have another child. And the night before…

Could they have already started?

Her gaze met his. He held on for all he was worth. Kept his eyes wide open.

And wondered if it would be a boy or a girl.

* * * * *

*Don't miss previous books in the
Sierra's Web miniseries,*

His Lost and Found Family
Reluctant Roommates

Available now from Harlequin Special Edition!

*And check out Sierra's story
in the online read prequel*

Trusting Her Betrayer

Available now on Harlequin.com!

Was she really considering allowing herself to be
captured by the man who'd killed Amber? Even though
he'd insisted he hadn't murdered Jeremy, how did she
know for sure? She could be putting herself into the
hands of a ruthless monster.

The sound of the back door opening cut into her
thoughts.

"Hey there," Trace said, dropping into the chair next
to her, one lock of his dark hair falling over his forehead.
He looked so damn handsome her chest ached. "Are you
okay? You look upset."

If he only knew.

HRSEXP0822

"Maybe a little," she admitted, well aware he'd see straight through her if she tried to claim she wasn't. In the short time they'd been together, she couldn't help but notice how attuned he'd become to her emotions. And she to his. Suddenly, she understood that if she really was going to go through with this risky plan, she wanted to make love to Trace one last time.

Moving quickly, before she allowed herself to doubt or rationalize, she turned to him. "I need you," she murmured, getting up and moving over to sit on his lap. His gaze darkened as she wrapped her arms around him. When she leaned in close and grazed her mouth across his, he met her kiss with the kind of blazing heat that made her lose all sense of rhyme or reason.

Don't miss
Protected by the Texas Rancher *by Karen Whiddon,*
available October 2022 wherever
Harlequin Romantic Suspense books and
ebooks are sold.

Harlequin.com

HARLEQUIN
PLUS

Announcing a **BRAND-NEW** multimedia subscription service for romance fans like you!

Read, Watch and Play.

Experience the easiest way to get the romance content you crave.

Start your **FREE 7 DAY TRIAL** at www.harlequinplus.com/freetrial.